Samuel E. Kiser

Budd Wilkins at the Show

Samuel E. Kiser

Budd Wilkins at the Show

ISBN/EAN: 9783744707961

Printed in Europe, USA, Canada, Australia, Japan

Cover: Foto ©Andreas Hilbeck / pixelio.de

More available books at **www.hansebooks.com**

"BUDD WILKINS AT THE SHOW,"

AND

OTHER VERSES.

❀ ❀ ❀

A COLLECTION OF POEMS FOR READERS
BOTH PUBLIC AND PRIVATE.

❀ ❀ ❀

SAMUEL ELLSWORTH KISER.

❀ ❀ ❀

THE HELMAN-TAYLOR COMPANY,
CLEVELAND, O.
1898.

INTRODUCTION....

Somebody has said that a book of poems should never be published without a good excuse. The present author thinks he has one. Many of the rhymes contained in this little volume have been printed and reprinted in the American newspapers, and many inquiries have come to the author from people who were good enough to express desires for his verses "in book form." Hence another tender foundling is placed upon the world's doorstep.

S. E. K.

Cleveland, Nov. 9th, 1898.

CONTENTS.

CHARACTER SKETCHES.

NATURE AND HER MOODS.

CONTENTS.

CONTENTS.

A Few Boys.

BUDD WILKINS AT THE SHOW.

Since I've got used to city ways and don't
    scare at the cars,
It makes me smile to set and think of
    years ago.—My stars!
How green I was, and how green all them
    country people be—
Sometimes it seems almost as if this hardly
    could be me.

Well, I was goin' to tell you 'bout Budd
    Wilkins: I declare
He was the durndest, greenest chap that
    ever breathed the air—
The biggest town on earth, he thought,
    was our old county seat,
With its one two-story brick hotel and
    dusty bizness street.

We'd fairs in fall and now and then a
    dance or huskin' bee,
Which was the most excitin' things Budd
    Wilkins ever see,
Until, one winter, Skigginsville was all
    turned upside down
By a troupe of real play actors a-comin'
    into town.

The court house it was turned into a the-
    ater, that night,

1

And I don't s'pose I'll live to see another
    sich a sight:
I guess that every person who was able fer
    to go
Jest natchelly cut loose fer oncet, and
    went to see the show.

Me and Budd we stood around there all
    day in the snow,
But gosh! it paid us, fer we got seats
    right in the second row!
Well, the brass band played a tune er two,
    and then the play begun,
And 'twa'n't long 'fore the villain had
    the hero on the run.

Say, talk about your purty girls with
    sweet, confidin' ways—
I never see the equal yit, in all o' my
    born days,
Of that there brave young heroine, so
    clingin' and so mild,
And jest as innocent as if she'd been a
    little child.

I most forgot to say that Budd stood six
    feet in his socks,
As brave as any lion, too, and stronger
    than an ox!
But there never was a man, I'll bet, that
    had a softer heart,
And he was always sure to take the
    weaker person's part.

Budd, he fell dead in love right off with
    that there purty girl,
And I suppose the feller's brain was in a
    fearful whirl,
Fer there he set and gazed at her, and
    when she sighed he sighed,
And when she hid her face and sobbed, he
    actually cried.

He clinched his fists and ground his teeth
    when the villain laid his plot
And said out loud he'd like to kill the
    rogue right on the spot,
And when the hero helped the girl, Budd
    up and yelled "Hooray!"
He'd clean fergot the whole blame thing
    was nothin' but a play.

At last the villain trapped the girl, that
    sweet confidin' child,
And when she cried fer help, why I'll
    admit that I was riled;
The hero couldn't do a thing, but roll and
    writhe around
And tug and groan because they'd got the
    poor chap gagged and bound.

The maiden cried: "Unhand me now,
    or, weak girl that I am—"
And then Budd Wilkins he jumped up
    and give his hat a slam,
And, quicker'n I can tell it he was up
    there raisin' Ned,
A-rescuin' the maiden and a-punchin' the
    rogue's head.

3

I can't, somehow, perticklerize concernin'
    that there row:
The whole thing seems a sort of blur as I
    recall it now—
But I can still remember that there was a
    fearful thud,
With the air chock full of arms and legs
    and the villain under Budd.

I never see a chap so bruised and battered
    up before
As that there villain was when he was
    picked up from the floor!—
The show? Oh, it was busted, and they
    put poor Budd in jail,
And kept him there all night, because I
    couldn't go his bail.

Next mornin' what d'you think we heard?
    Most s'prised in all my life!
That sweet confidin' maiden was the cruel
    villain's wife!
Budd wilted when he heard it, and he
    groaned, and then, says he:
"Well, I'll be dummed! Bill, that's the
    last play actin' show fer me!"

VISITING LAURA BELLE.

I've just been up to town to see my
    daughter Laura Belle—
She married Henry Lee, you know—
    they're doin' mighty well!
Live right in style, I tell you, in a house
    that's big enough
For half a dozen fam'lies most, and oh
    the piles of stuff
That they've got scattered through it,
    sich as bricky-brack 'nd books,
And they're keepin' "first" and "second"
    girls 'nd chambermaids 'nd cooks,
And kerridges 'nd all sich like, 'nd she
    wears diamond rings—
I vow, it must make Henry hump to pay
    fer all them things!

And they are in society, clean over head
    'nd all—
Card parties 'nd receptions, 'nd now and
    then a ball,
And operies 'nd dinners at the club—gosh!
    I dunno
How folks can do much work 'nd be for-
    ever on the go;
And I told Henry plain that this here
    bein' out at night

5

And sleepin' late next mornin' wasn't
    altogether right.
But he paid no attention 'cept to sort of
    draw up straight
And say in kind of sneerin' tones, "Some
    folks was out of date."

Now, that makes me remember what I
    started out to say:
I didn't notice it at first, but seemed,
    from day to day,
As if they had a notion that I wa'n't the
    proper style,
Because when comp'ny come they kept
    me busy all the while
A tendin' to the children, in the nursery,
    upstairs,
And they never took me out to no society
    affairs,
And in a lot of ways I seen that they
    appeared to be—
Well, what's the use to hold it back?
    They was ashamed of me!

Excuse me—I've ketched cold, I guess—I
    wonder what I done
With that there henkerchief of mine—
    gosh, how my nose doos run!
I can't help thinkin' of the time when
    Laura Belle and me
Was just like two old cronies! She would
    set upon my knee,
And I would teach her pieces, 'nd hug
    her to my heart,

6

And tell her that some day I s'posed
    some man 'ud make us part,
And then she'd always kiss me 'nd look
    up at me 'nd say
That I was all the beau for her, 'nd she'd
    never go away.

And when her mother died I mind how
    she held up so brave,
And kept me from a breakin' down right
    there beside the grave,
And when we got back home agin, where
    all appeared so bare
And empty like 'nd lonesome, just 'cause
    mother wasn't there,
She come 'nd put her arms around my
    neck, 'nd then we cried
Together there right on the spot, almost,
    where mother died!
Oh Lord, I don't know why it was—but I
    could plainly see,
When I was there, that Laura Belle was
    sort of 'shamed of me!

I s'pose I am old-fashioned, 'nd Henry
    may be right
About my bein' out of date, 'nd mebby
    I'm a sight—
But I ain't never robbed no man, nor
    cheated no one yit,
And I have never took a thing I couldn't
    fairly git,
But in the city things like them don't seem
    to count fer much—

7

They honor people fer their bonds 'nd
    railroad stocks 'nd such,
And for the servants they can keep, 'nd
    the costly clo's they wear—
They haven't any kind of use fer such as
    me, up there!

I'm glad to be at home agin—back here
    upon the place
Where I was born, 'nd where I'm not
    afraid to show my face—
Here where I'm just as good as any one
    that I may meet,
And where I do not have to walk behind
    folks in the street!
I wish that I'd not went up there at all,
    'nd that I had
My little Laura Belle agin, to love 'nd pet
    her dad,
As long ago she used to—but no! that
    cannot be—
Oh Lord, it breaks my heart to think that
    she's ashamed of me!

LITTLE KATE.

"Well, daughter, you, of course, should
    know the best about your name;
If Kathryn's what will suit you best, why
    then adopt the same;
You've been away to college, and I s'pose
    you've learned a lot,
And you ought to have as fine a name as
    any girl has got.

"No, I don't say you mustn't change to
    Kathryn—not at all,
The difference, as far as I can see, is very
    small—
But, lawsy me! I can't, somehow, keep
    back the tears to-day—
I guess it's cause you look so much like
    her that's gone away.

"And, speakin' of your mother, dear, it
    seems as if I jest
Could see her lyin' there again, with you
    upon her breast—
Ah, what a glad look filled her eyes when
    I bent down and said
I'd call our baby after her—jest 'fore her
    spirit fled

"I s'pose that I'm old fogyish—that I'm
    'way out of date,

9

And that it's foolishness for me to want
    to call you Kate;
But that's the name that she went by—a
    name that's dear to me,
And when I call you by it I keep fresh her
    memory.

"Yes, daughter, change to Kathryn, if
    that name will suit you best,
But we called you Kate the day you lay
    asleep upon her breast—
There, there, my dear, don't cry no more
    —you ain't a bit to blame—
I knew your heart was true to her and
    that you'd keep her name."

WHEN DAD GOT RELIGION.

I ain't no hand to argy; never could
    remember dates,
And that's a fatal failin' for a feller that
    debates;
I don't, jist now, remember whether
    Moses up and smote
The rock before or after Noah sailed off
    in his boat;
I know that little David knocked the giant
    feller out,
But I've gone and clean forgotten what
    the trouble was about!
The Bible's full of chapters that I never
    understood,
But there's one thing I am sure of: that
    religion's mighty good!

My step-dad used to be a man that every-
    body feared;
The very old horned devil had got in him,
    it appeared;
He used to knock poor mother down and
    drag her by the hair,
And if I bared my back to-day, you'd see
    his trade marks there!
I couldn't help but trimble if he'd even
    look my way,

11

And that'd make him angry, and, great
    grief! the things he'd say!
On many a night when he was out and I
    had went to bed,
My mother'd kneel beside me and we'd
    wish that we was dead!

One winter they got up a big revival
    meetin' there—
Church was packed—it seemed that we'd
    religion in the air!
Mourner's bench was crowded every night
    for many a week;
I tell you it'd raise your hair to hear that
    preacher speak!
He'd make you think that Satan was right
    there behind your back,
To git you if you didn't take the straight
    and narrow track!
Night after night I laid awake, afraid to
    close my eyes,
For fear I might get took because I'd
    been a-tellin' lies.

Seemed as if dad looked jist like the
    preacher pictured out
The old boy, in them sermons—but I
    'magined it, no doubt;
And, one night, when he come and stood
    beside the trundle-bed,
I thought he meant to beat me, and I
    covered up my head;
And then I laid and trimbled! I could
    seem to feel his blows,

But purty soon I felt him gently pullin' at
    the clo's,
And when I bared my face agin and
    looked up at him, he
Stood there awhile and cried, and then
    knelt down and prayed fer me.

He never whipped me after that, nor
    scolded me no more,
And I never knowed that life was half as
    beautiful before;
All the world seemed brighter; it appeared
    as if the sun
Had got to shinin' fairer and a new world
    had begun!
I'm not no smart theologist that's got the
    facts all pat
Concernin' sects and creeds and forms and
    all sich things as that,
The Bible's full of passages I never under-
    stood,
But there's one thing I am sure of:
    that religion's mighty good!

AN EASY MAN.

Never seen an easier man in all my livin'
    days
Than my old neighbor, Lisha Green, nor
    sich slow-goin' ways!
Knowed him from his boyhood up—always
    jist the same,
Never seemed to care a cent—took things
    as they came;
In the spring when other folks would git
    to breakin' ground,
Lisha'd wait fer fairer days, and jist keep
    settin' round.

Farm his father left him was the finest
    thereabout,
But fences soon got shaky and the weeds
    begin to sprout;
Buildin's got to leakin' and the crops they
    wouldn't grow—
Plastered on a mor'gage—then the cattle
    had to go!—
Still he didn't mind it, and no one ever
    found
Lisha doin' anything but merely settin'
    'round.

Sort of dried up—Lisha did—and one day
    blowed away,

Leavin' nothin' back of him but lots of
  debts to pay.
Guess he's up in heaven now—hope he is,
  at least—
Know he never purposely done harm to
  man or beast!—
Mebby he's got golden wings—mebby he
  is crowned—
Bet his wings are folded though and that
  he's settin' round.

DEACON WHITE'S CONFESSION.

I've always been a Christian man and
    tried to live upright,
But Satan laid a hidjeous plan fer me the
    other night:
I went up to the wicked town to see my
    nephew Dick,
And there became the victim of a low-
    down, wicked trick!
And here I stand in meetin' to confess the
    whole affair—
I've got to ease my conscience fer a
    weight is restin' there—
And I'll tell it as it happened, of the
    dancin' girl and all,
And I hope that you'll forgive me, fer the
    best of us may fall.

You know when Dick was but a child, his
    folks they died, and so
I had to take and raise 'im till a little
    while ago;
And since he's been up there he's rose
    uncommon fast, they say,
But I'm afraid he's started out upon an
    evil way.
I used to think that Dick was just as good
    as he could be,

And how I loved to feel that he was like a
    son to me!
But I'm afraid 'twas all put on, fer other-
    wise he'd not
Have put his uncle into such a fix as I
    have got.

Him and a friend of his they said they had
    a treat in store,
"The likes of which dear Uncle Ned had
    never seen before!"
Well, they was right concernin' that! It
    was oncommon new—
I hardly knowed where I was at, before
    the thing was through.
A gaudy place it was, and we set up there
    where the folks
Upon the stage could look at me and use
    me fer their jokes—
They talked about my whiskers and they
    called me "Rube" and "Josh,"
And kept repeatin', all the time,
    "B'golly!" and "B'gosh!"

At last a girl come out to sing—as purty
    as could be—
But she didn't hardly wear a thing, as fur
    as I could see.
Immejitly she turned to us and then let
    loose a kick
That made my senses teeter jus' as if I
    had been sick!
And then she romped and danced and
    sung and tore around awhile—

But I set stiff and solemn like and never
    cracked a smile—
And so she kept agoin' on the worst I
    ever saw,
Till, finally, she says to me: "You ain't
    mad, are you, paw?"

Then everybody laughed, and Dick he
    punched me in the side
And him and that there friend of his
    howled till they nearly died.
And 'fore I knowed jus' what was up, the
    girl was there with me
A-pullin' of my whiskers as familiar as
    could be!
She called me "paw" and "baby," and
    she chucked me on the chin—
And me a-knowin' all the time it was a
    wicked sin—
But what, I ask you, bretherun—I ask
    it face to face—
Could anyone of you have done had you
    been in my place?

They ordered up the wine, them two; I
    heard the glasses chink,
And not another thing would do but I
    must take a drink!
The stuff it burned like poison! Her
    breath was on my cheek—
But deep, deep down inside of me, I heard
    a small voice speak!
And, jumpin' up, I hollered that I'd got
    enough of that,

And so I simply bolted, without either
    coat or hat,
And I run as if Old Nick himself was
    comin' on behind—
With a weight upon my conscience and a
    blur upon my mind!

And here I stand a penitent before you all
    to-day—
I know I oughtn't to have went to see no
    kind of play—
But I have prayed and I have wept! I'll
    go to town no more,
And, in my heart, I'm jus' as free from
    evil as before.   *   *
Ah, thank you for your gracious words!
    They lift me from the dust!
I raise my head again and take my stand
    among the just!
I've told it to you truly, of the dancin'
    girl and all—
I knowed that you'd forgive me, fer the
    best of us may fall!

GRANDMA'S LAMENT.

When we lived on the farm, pa used to get
    up with the sun,
And prophesyin' weather was the first
    thing that he done!
He'd straighten up and stretch hisself
    and yawn awhile and blink,
And then he'd say! "It'll rain to-day,"
    or "Clearin' up, I think!"
He had a hundred signs, or more, by
    which he always told
If it was goin' to shine or pour, or turn
    out hot or cold.

But others come to live upon the old place
    long ago.
(Dear, how I'd like to be there now, to
    see the peach trees blow!)
And pa he's lost his knack of tellin' what
    it's goin' to do
Since we've got settled here in town,
    where everything's so new;
When he gets up o' mornin's now first
    thing he's sure to say
Is: "Mother, where's the paper? What's
    the weather fer to-day?"

Land sakes! I don't. know what this
    world is surely comin' to!

They don't appear to be a thing 'lectricity
    won't do!
It'll tell the weather days ahead; it's took
    the horse's place,
And everybody knows just how it's wiped
    out time and space!
They's scasely any day goes by but some
    inventor finds
Some new and startlin' thing to do to
    upset people's minds.

But human nature ain't improved, as fur
    as I can see,
And folks are even colder now than what
    they used to be;
Each man jest tries, with all his might, to
    git some other downed,
It's got to be a general fight among 'em
    all around!
The rich are richer than they were; the
    poor are poorer, too—
And if you want to shine in church,
    you've got to rent a pew.

I'm tired of it and I wish that I could
    wake, my dears,
Some day and find that things had all
    rolled back 'bout thirty years;
That all this rush had been a dream—that
    we was still out there,
With the cows a-windin' down the lane
    and sweet smells in the air,
And pa a-stretchin' hisself again in that
    old honest way,
And sayin' lovin'-like to me: "Yes, it'll
    be fair, to-day!"

"Come, Betsy, let's be cheerful, 'tain't no
    use to set 'nd fret;
I know the crops look ragged, but they
    may turn out well yet;
Your rheumatis' is hurtin', 'nd my back
    is stiff 'nd sore,
But let's hope it's somethin' better that
    to-morrow has in store—
You know that when the light comes, it is
    darkest just before.

"Of course, I'm not pretendin' that the
    cares what we have had
Was as deep as this one is, but some of
    them was purty bad,
'Nd to-morrow—there's no tellin'—we
    may hear from John by then,
'Nd find that he's recovered 'nd gone
    back to work again."
The weeping mother murmured some-
    thing like a low "Amen!"

The morrow came, and with it came a
    letter—not the one
That they longed for and had prayed for,
    yet it told them of their son.
The father wiped his glasses and read,
    and then reread—

It seemed as if some weighty thing had
    struck him on the head—
For the words were staring at him, and
    they told him John was dead!

"Well, mother, he is comin'," thus the old
    man spake at last;
"The sickness that was on 'im's gone, the
    danger point is past,
'Nd he's comin' home to-morrow—
    comin' back here fer to stay"—
She hurried to the kitchen, and old Jasper
    heard her say:—
"Kill a chicken, he'll be hungry after
    travelin' all day."

UNCLE HENRY'S DOWNFALL.

It takes all kinds of people to make up the
    world, they say,
And I've met a mighty lot of different
    species, in my day—
All with their various hobbies and their
    politics and creeds,
The things that poison one may be just
    what some other needs;
One man'll claim you can't be saved unless
    you've been immersed,
While the next one says of all the foolish
    doctrines, that's the worst—
What one man likes another scorns, that
    seems to be the rule,
And the chap that tries to please 'em all
    is just a common fool.

Some folks can't stand the climate here
    and want to move away,
While others think it's lovely—or, at
    least, that's what they say;
One man'll read a story and he'll split his
    sides and roar,
While the next one mebby'll say he never
    see such rot before;
Some people go to meetin' every Sunday,
    rain or clear,

While other fellers hardly hear a sermon
    once a year—
What one man likes his neighbor has no
    use for, as a rule,
And the man that tries to please 'em all
    is just a common fool.

When you think the weather's pleasant
    the first fellow that you meet,
As like as not'll grumble at the cold or
    else the heat;
They made me school director here about
    a year ago,
And I started out intendin' to give every
    one a show;
I tried to keep from takin' sides—I done
    the best I could—
Last week they kicked me out and said I
    wasn't any good!
I guess that every other man is cranky,
    as a rule,
And the chap that tries to please 'em all's
    an ordinary fool!

THE MISSING ONE.

I don't think I'll go in to town to see the
    boys come back;
My bein' there would do no good in all
    that jam and pack;
There'll be enough to welcome them—to
    cheer them, when they come
A-marchin' bravely to the time that's beat
    upon the drum;
They'll never miss me in the crowd—not
    one of 'em will care
If, when the cheers are ringin' loud, I'm
    not among them there.

I went to see them march away, I hollered
    with the rest,
And didn't they look fine that day
    a-marchin' four abreast,
With my boy James up near the front, as
    handsome as could be,
And wavin' back a fond farewell to
    mother and to me!
I vow my old knees trimbled so when they
    had all got by,
I had to jist set down upon the curbstone
    there and cry.

And now they're comin' home agen! The
    record that they won

Was sich as shows we still have men when
    men's work's to be done!
There wasn't one of 'em that flinched—
    each feller stood the test—
Wherever they were sent they sailed right
    in and done their best!
They didn't go away to play; they
    knowed what was in store;
But there's a grave somewhere, to-day,
    down on the Cuban shore!

I guess that I'll not go to town to see the
    boys come in;
I don't jist feel like mixin' up in all that
    crush and din!
There'll be enough to welcome them—to
    cheer them when they come
A-marchin' bravely to the time that's beat
    upon the drum.
And the boys'll never notice—not a one
    of 'em will care,
For the soldier that would miss me ain't
    a-goin' to be there!

"THEY'VE NAMED HIM
AFTER ME."

I never liked that Amos Gray,
    Somehow he seemed to be
A sort of schemer in his way
    And so it bothered me
Like sixty when he started home from
    church, one Sunday night,
With our Alice, and they sot, without a
    spark o' light,
A-talkin' and a-laughin' till
    Away past one o'clock,
With ma a-frettin' fit to kill,
    And me as mad's a hawk!

You see I've got the finest place
    In this hull township, and
The way I figgered out the case
    Young Gray had simply planned
To marry in the fambly and take hold and
    run affairs,
And so I told him plainly that we seen his
    cunnin' snares!
If him and Alice had to go
    And marry, well and good,
But I took care to let him know
    How matters reely stood!

28

'Course Alice praised him up and cried
 And got her mother won,
And then they both pitched in and tried
 To git me on the run,
But I had took my stand and there I
 vowed that I would stay,
And so, one day the words was said and
 the young folks went away!
 My grief! how lonesome it did seem
 When Alice wa'n't about;
 Sometimes I wanted jist to scream
 To chase the silence out.

Well, that was 'bout a year ago,
 And last night Amos he
Come tearin' down to let us know
 They'd named him after me—
I mean the little boy they've got—I've
 jist been up with wife,
And I never seen as fine a child as him in
 all my life!
 And smart! By George, when I stood
 there,
 As quiet as could be,
 He woke and smiled—he did—I
 swear!—
 And they've named him after me!

They say he's got my chin and nose,
 His eyes are like mine, too;
From his curly head clear to his toes,
 He's like me through and through!
I'm goin' up to town to-day, to deed the
 farm away,

I'm tired workin' and I give the place to
        Amos Gray;
    We'll all live here and part no more,
    I've got 'em to agree—
Say, did I mention it before?
    They've named him after me!

ONLY A WOMAN.

He used to treat her shameful! I have
    heard the neighbors say
That they wouldn't think of usin' a com-
    mon cur that way!
Let her slave until her back ached and
    her fingers fairly bled,
And once he throwed a hatchet that jist
    barely missed her head!
She would do a hard day's sewin', and
    then he'd come home at night
And abuse her if the supper didn't happen
    to be right.

She might of married better, for she used
    to be as sweet
And as fair a little maiden as a feller'd
    care to meet;
Her cheeks was round and rosy, and her
    eyes'd set you wild,
And the world seemed mighty pleasant
    when she looked at you and smiled!
Had an ankle that was lovely, and her
    form was plump and trim—
And everybody wondered when she went
    and married him.

I s'pose she thought, like other foolish
    girls have thought before,

That she'd make him quit his drinkin',
    but he only drunk the more—
Went from bad to worse the minute that
    she'd given him her hand,
And the way she'd stick up for him I
    could never understand—
Law, she'd flare up like a wildcat when
    her folks'd interfere—
But, alas, her girlish beauty soon begun
    to disappear!

One night, they say, he choked her—Gol,
    I wish that I'd been there!—
Knocked her down and beat and dragged
    her round the kitchen by the hair!
And so, with tears a-streamin' down her
    face, she went away
To the home in which she hadn't set a
    foot for many a day—
Went and laid her achin' head upon her
    weepin' mother's breast—
Meekly went and sobbed and snuggled in
    the old home nest.

After while we seen the roses bloomin' on
    her cheeks agin,
And she hadn't lost the purty little dimple
    from her chin,
And in spite of all the sorrow and the
    troubles she'd been through
She was jist as sweet as ever—and a little
    sweeter, too!—
And the folks begin to gossip, as you
    know, folks always will,

And wonder why she didn't hurry up and
    get a bill.

He kept on, when she had left him, in his
    old disgraceful way;
No one knew jist how he managed—but
    it leaked out yisterday
That he'd got some sort of fever, and in
    order to git through,
He'd have to have a doctor and some
    tender nursin', too!—
O she smiled at me, one mornin', and the
    whole world seemed to swim!
She is lovelier than ever—but she's goin'
    back to him!

UNCLE RUFUS IN THE CITY.

Been a-livin' in town with my boy James,
    now goin' on 'leven years,
But I ain't got used to it yit, by gum!
    This city life appears
To jest knock all your energy out,
    'N' leave you sort of dead!
I'm too blame tired to git about,
    'N' I've a buzzin' in my head!
I guess it's the noise of the cars 'n' things
    that rings in my ears all day,
'N', oh but I wish I could eat 'n' sleep in
    the good, old-fashioned way!

I'd like to be back on the farm agin,
    where the buds is sproutin' now,
'N', Lord, how I'd like to rise with the
    sun 'n' git out behind the plow!
Turnin' the mellow furrow along
    Up over the slopin' hill,
'N' hearin' some farm hand's happy song
    Mixed up with his "Haw, there, Bill!"
Seein' the crows a-circlin' round, way up
    in the clear blue sky,
'N' hearin' mother blowin' the horn fer
    breakfast, by 'n' by.

I'd like to stop at the end of the field 'n'
    feel the country breeze,

As it comes through the orchard on the
    hill with the scent of the bloomin'
    trees;
'N' I'd like to smell the sweet wood smoke
    That comes from the burnin' brush,
'N' instead of the sparrow's tiresome
    croak
    I'd hear the song of the thrush!
'N', then, to wash in the old tin pail
    with mother standin' there—
What's this? Tears tricklin' down my
    face? Well, I'm cryin', I declare!

I've lost my appetite, somehow, since I
    ain't got nothin' to do,
'N' the days jest seem to come because
    they've got to be worried through!
Out yonder the trees are in blossom now,
    As they blossomed when I was there;
But some one else is guidin' the plow
    'N' breathin' the scented air,
'N' mother's asleep on the grassy hill
    beneath the poplar tree—
'N' I wish the leaves it's puttin' forth was
    also to shelter me!

BENEATH OLD GLORY.

I was down to the postoffice 'tother day,
Settin' there and whittlin' away
   While Hammond sorted the letters,
When all of a sudden it come to me
How happy a feller ought to be
That's born in this glorious land of the
     free,
   Where no one kneels to his betters.

There was the flag above my head,
With the stars and the blue and the white
     and the red,
   And I watched it float and flutter;
And it made me proud to know that I
Was as good as any man under the sky
And wasn't compelled to help supply
   Some prince's bread and butter.

But presently Silas Gifford he
Come strollin' along and set down by me,
   And then he begin to grumble:
Nothin' seemed to be goin' right,
Potatoes were poor and corn was a sight—
Wheat had been injured by the blight,
   And rye had taken a tumble.

I whittled away and listened awhile,
And then says I: "Look here now, Sile,
   What's the use of your frettin'?

Look at the starry flag up there;
Look at them stripes wave in the air—
Man, think what it is to be settin' where
  You're lucky enough to be settin'!"

He set and looked and I heard him sigh,
And I saw his face flush, by and by—
  He'd forgotten his doleful story;
And then he stood up and he says to me:
"Lord, ain't it great," he says, "to be
    free—
To be an American"—says he—
  "And stand beneath Old Glory!"

AN EVERY-DAY WONDER.

I've lived in this here world of ours, now,
    sixty years and more,
And things don't seem to strike me just
    as they have heretofore;
I've been a-thinkin' hard about a lot of
    things of late,
And folks I once despised I sort of look
    upon as great.

For instance, there is old De Gull, who's
    owin' every one;
I used to hold him up as an example for
    to shun,
But though he's deep down in the hole,
    just see the way he lives,
And think of all the parties and the
    charity he gives!

I work for what I have, and don't owe
    any man a dime,
While he rides 'round in carriages, and
    has a gorgeous time;
He goes in high society and lives 'most
    like a king,
While folks don't think that I amount to
    scarcely anything.

Now, what I wanted to get at was some-
    thing like this here:

It takes a genius to be a fraud, and yet
    appear
As if he was the greatest man a person
    ever saw,
Who makes the folks he owes stand off
    and gaze at him in awe.

They say that story 'bout the whale and
    Jonah isn't true.
And now they've gone—the preachers
    have—and tackled David, too;
They say he didn't write the Psalms, at
    least, not nearly all—
I wonder what'll be the next good old
    belief to fall?

They've even thrown suspicion on the
    birth of Moses, and
The princess who discovered him down
    there in Egypt land—
They say there ain't no fiery lake, no
    devil, therefore no
Such place as that which used to make
    the sinners tremble so.

They've said that Noah's ark is just a
    piece of fiction, too,
And that the tale of Daniel in the lion's
    den ain't true;
They've said that Adam's just a myth,
    they've said the same of Eve—
I wonder if there's anything they'll leave
    us to believe?

They ridicule old Joshua for pointin' at
    the sun,

And tellin' it to stop—they say the thing
    was never done;
They've taken up the patriarchs and ques-
    tioned all their acts;
They say the Bible's quite a book, but
    rather shy of facts.

Well, let 'em preach and let 'em lay the
    whole great structure low!
I s'pose they have to talk that way 'cause
    people want it so;
The good book doesn't suit some folks at
    all, but as for me—
I'm satisfied to keep the faith I got at
    mother's knee.

You know there's always someone in each
    neighborhood that stands
Above the other people, for his fam'ly or
    his lands,
Or because he's reely smart enough to jist
    go right ahead
And take the lead in ev'rything that's
    ever done or said,
For folks, in that respect, are like the
    quackin' geese that fly
Behind some knowin' gander as they trail
    across the sky—
From the army to the hay field it's the
    same the whole way through,
There must always be a leader if there's
    anything to do.

Well, the man who sort of run things
    down in our neighborhood
Was a feller by the name of—let's see—
    s'pose we call 'im Wood;
He owned three of the finest farms within
    a dozen miles,
And the common supposition was that he
    had wealth in piles,
And in addition to them things, he
    measured six foot one,

And had a reputation for the fightin' he
    had done—   .
Moreover, he'd a daughter, jist as hand-
    some as a rose,
Who, at the age of twenty-one, had forty-
    'leven beaux.

One day there come along a chap from
    York State who began
To work for Henry Holman—sort of
    quiet, slender man
Along somewhere about the age of
    twenty-three or four,
And Nellie Wood soon tired of the beaux
    she'd had before;
But jist about the time that her and this
    young man agreed
That they had ought to marry, her old
    dad decided he'd
Step in and take a hand! Ordered John
    to vanish, nor never come agen—
Said his girl could have her pick of fifty
    better men.

But they kept on a-lovin' and a-meetin'
    here and there,
And, of course, the busy-bodies had to
    follow the affair,
Until one evenin' John was at the
    Corners, in the store,
When suddenly there was a hush, for
    loomin' in the door
Was Nellie's dad about as mad as any
    man could get,

And he went for that young feller like a
    hurricane, you bet!
He didn't stop to argue, nor to throw his
    coat aside,
But, without a word of warnin' started in
    to tan his hide.

They say that kegs and boxes was sent
    whirlin' ev'rywhere,
And that legs and arms and coat tails was
    a-spinnin' in the air;
They was rippin', they was tearin', they
    was whiskers floatin' round,
They sent the show-case flyin', and spilled
    groceries by the pound;
They tumbled over barrels and they ham-
    mered, till, at last
John got the old man under where he
    held him hard and fast—
Held him there and choked him—then,
    without a word to say
Got up and brushed his clothin' and
    serenely walked away.

Of course you know what happened then—
    John took the girl and went,
But they didn't, like so many do, come
    back home penitent;
He got a job in town and 'twa'n't so very
    long before
We heard the feller'd went and bought an
    interest in a store.
But Nellie's dad, he, somehow, had the
    hardest kind of luck,

From that time on, that any man in this
    world ever struck—
Everything he touched jist seemed to go
    to pieces, and
'Twa'n't long before they took away the
    last rod of his land.

Let's see—it's 'leven years since I come
    in to town to stay—
My cracky! how the months and years do
    seem to slip away!
I guess the time has passed so fast because
    I've never had
Sich happiness as this since she was here
    to make me glad—
I mean my daughter's mother, who had
    died long, long before
The episode I mentioned which occurred
    there in the store,
And the little grassy mound upon the
    hillside where she lies
Is the only thing that makes me like to
    keep up the old ties.   *   *   *

Yes, the names that I've referred to was
    to throw you off the track;
It was me that got the lickin' and was all
    tore up the back,
And my son-in-law's the smartest little
    man in this here town,
With something like a half a million dollars
    salted down!
And him and Nellie's jist like two young
    spoonin' lovers yet,

Enjoyin' all the comforts that good
    money's made to get,
With their little ones around them, all
    as happy as can be,
And makin' this old world a reg'lar
    Paradise fer me!

THE MAN WHO ONLY SMILED.

I never saw a man as free from what is
    known as care
As Ira Hamlin used to be—it seemed to
    me, I swear,
Sometimes, as if the feller must jist laugh
    the whole day through
And keep his smilin' up at night, while
    he was sleepin', too;
Never used to meet him but he'd have a
    word to say
To kind of cheer a feller up and drive the
    blues away.

I mind the time his horse was killed—the
    best one that he had—
He never gave a sign to show that he was
    feelin' bad;
Jist kept a smilin' countenance and
    worked away the same
As if he'd lost a nickel in a friendly little
    game;
Nothin' seemed to break him down;
    always crackin' jokes—
Makin' light of things that would have
    worried other folks.

One fall his boy was taken sick—none of
    the doctors knew

Jist what the trouble was, and so he lay
    all winter through
A-hoverin' 'twixt life and death—still Ira
    smiled away—
Always had his joke, or else a hopeful
    word to say.—
But when the trees began to bud and the
    birds began to mate
They laid his little boy away, up by the
    graveyard gate.

We watched 'im, as he stood beside the
    little grave up there,
But no one saw 'im shed a tear—he
    didn't seem to care—
And when the last words had been said,
    he simply turned away,
And went about his work again, with not
    a word to say—
A-smilin' as he always had, and, in a day
    or so,
A-jokin' as if sorrow was a thing he didn't
    know.

Well, I jist couldn't stand it! He was
    plowin' on the hill:
At first I says: "No, what's the use?"
    and then says I: "I will!"—
So I went up, and we set down, upon the
    old wood sled,
And he began to crack his jokes, and then
    I up and said
I couldn't, fer the life of me, see how
    'twas any one

48

Could throw his burdens off and go ahead,
 as he had done.

"I don't believe," says I, "that you are
 built like other folks:
I've never seen you feelin' blue—you're
 always crackin' jokes;
Don't sorrow never git into your breast
 and rankle there?
Or has the Good Lord made you so you
 never have a care?—
But Ira'd put his face into his hands and
 bent his head,
And I'd a given all the world to take back
 what I said.

I never heard such sobs before! We set
 there half a day,
And never said a single word, for he jist
 wept away;
Seemed as if the sorrow he'd escaped in
 former years
Had all come on 'im in a flood, and same
 way with his tears;
But when, at last he'd wiped his eyes,
 he turned around to me,
And then between his sobs, in sort of
 chokin' words, says he:

"I've tried to keep a cheerful face,
 because I didn't care
To burden other folks with woes that God
 gave me to bear;

They've troubles of their own; I thought
    that smilin' was the best,
Yet often when I've laughed 'twas jist to
    ease my achin' breast—
But now, it seems, you want a man to
    mope and moan and groan,
Instead of keepin' back his tears till he
    can be alone—

*   *   *   *   *   *   *   *

I'd nothin' more to say, and so that night
    when all was still
I hunted out the little grave up yonder on
    the hill,
And there I stopped beside the gate and
    leaned against the bars,
And saw him kneelin' by the mound and
    lookin' toward the stars.

MA'S BOY, ART.

Have you ever seen it stormin' when it
    seemed that every tree
Would be ripped up by the roots, and all
    the furies were set free?
When the earth jist fairly trimbled under
    angry Nature's wrath,
And destruction seemed in store for every
    object in 'er path?
When the rain come down so hard the
    drops appeared to have been sent
Like rattlin' shot hurled out of some
    destructive instrument?—
Well, that's about the sort of mood that
    dad was in the day
That him and Arthur quarreled, and the
    latter went away.

"Don't never dare to set your foot inside
    my door again!"
Them were the words dad shouted, and
    his face was livid then.
And Art was full of foolish pride—he
    grabbed his hat and went—
He scorned the bill dad offered him—he
    wouldn't take a cent!
He wouldn't be beholdin' for a thing to
    dad, he swore—

It seems to me I see him now, a-standin'
    in the door,
With mother hangin' on his neck—and,
    oh, her piercin' cry!
For full a month I don't believe her eyes
    were ever dry!

We plowed and planted and we hoed—the
    summer wore away,
And every night when bedtime come, and
    mother knelt to pray,
I'd hear her ask the Lord to send his
    richest blessin' down
Upon her boy, away alone, up in the
    wicked town!
And often she would look at dad, with
    pleadin' eyes that said
The words she didn't dare to speak; but
    he would shake his head,
And close his lips, and clinch his fists, and
    then she'd hide 'er face,
And a sort of lonesome sadness seemed to
    hang around the place.

Such crops as seemed worth harvestin' we
    put away, some how;
We hadn't more than hay enough to half
    fill up a mow—
But we raised a flock of turkeys that was
    far the best around!—
We'd a gobbler dad declared would tip the
    scale at forty pound:
"I'll try to sell the others off Thanksgivin'
    week," he said,

"But I'm goin' to keep that gobbler, and
    we won't chop off his head!
Somehow, I kind of like the way he lords
    it with the rest,
For a heart is good, but still I like a
    haughty spirit best!"

The day before Thanksgivin' come, and
    dad drove down the lane;
The wind was raw, and sleety drops come
    rattlin' on the pane,
And mother set there thinkin'—then she
    give a frightened start—
The door was softly opened, and I looked,
    and there was Art,
So white and thin and haggard that, at
    first it seemed almost
As if it couldn't be himself, but just his
    hungry ghost—
And mother! Oh, her voice is still these
    many, many years,
But the cry she give rings just as plain as
    ever in my ears!

That afternoon, when dad come home,
    Art hid away, up stairs,
And mother bustled 'round and tried to
    not expose affairs,
But dad was hardly in the house before he
    stopped and said:
' What's goin' on? I want the truth!
    I'm not a punkin' head!"
Then mother, trimblin' like a leaf, ketched
    hold of Arthur's hand,

And led him slowly to the spot where dad
    had took his stand—
And Art stood there and looked at dad,
    and dad looked back at Art,
And mother prayed in whispers for the
    Lord to touch his heart.

It seemed an hour that they stood—then
    mother she give way:
"He's starved and sick," she cried to
    dad, "please say that he can stay!"
At last, dad turned, without a word, and
    left the room, and then
We set and wondered till, at last, we
    heard his step again.
He'd gone and killed the gobbler—he
    brought him in and said:
"He had a splendid spirit, and he held a
    haughty head—
But his head is low, at present, and he's
    lost his spirit, too—
How about Thanksgivin', mother? I'll
    jist leave it all to you."

THE HIRED MAN'S CONFESSION.

I got to thinkin' t'other day, about this
    world's affairs;
How some folks have it easy, and how
    some are bent with cares;
How some must work from mornin' till
    the sun sinks in the West,
And other people only do the things that
    suit 'em best—
I set there while the horses switched the
    buzzin' flies away,
And I thought how I had got to keep
    a-slavin' every day,
While them wealthy summer boarders
    that had come to us from town,
Spent the money that their dads, no
    doubt, had earned and salted down.

And, referrin' to them boarders, there is
    one among 'em who
Is the beautifullest maiden any mortal
    ever knew;
Oh, her voice is just like music and she's
    got an angel's face,
And since she come she's sort of made a
    heaven of the place,
And I've often set and watched her and
    then wished that I could be

Rich and handsome like them others, so
    that she would notice me—
But, of course, I'm just a farmer, with
    big, bony, calloused hands,
Only fit to love in secret every spot on
    which she stands.

And while I set there, thinkin', she come
    poppin' in my mind,
And then I got to dreamin' and my cares
    were left behind—
Got to thinkin' of myself as rich and
    handsome and forgot
All about the tired horses standin' out
    there in the lot!
But that couldn't last forever, there was
    work I had to do,
And I dropped down out of Cloudland,
    wishin' all of it was true,
And I rose up where I'd rested, in the
    corner by the tree,
And my heart stood still, for she was
    standin' there in front of me!

I don't know how it happened, but we
    stood there in the shade,
And I said a lot of things that sounded
    foolish, I'm afraid—
At least, I know I told her how I'd got to
    slave away,
And how I'd planned to go and get a job
    in town some day—
How I'd like to have white hands and dress
    in stylish clothin', too,

How I'd like to go and mingle with the
    people that she knew!
And how my face was burnin', and my
    heart, oh, how it beat!
And all the while she stood there, gazin'
    straight down at her feet.

After while she looked up at me, and I
    never shall forget
How sad and sweet her smile was and
    I hear her talkin' yet!
"You must work, it is your fortune, and
    your hands are big and bruised,
But to work is only manly—" them's the
    very words she used—
"And the man whose hands are softest
    and whose clothing is the best
Doesn't always have the bravest, purest
    heart within his breast;
You must work, while over yonder men
    put in their time at play,
But to me you're worth a dozen of those
    others, any day."

Then she shook my hand and left me, and
    I took the reins agen,
And workin', somehow, seemed to be all
    fired easy then!
Of course, I know she only said them
    words to ease my mind,
Said 'em only, heaven bless 'er, 'cause she
    wanted to be kind,
But although I know I never could expect
    that such as she

57

Would forsake the world she lives in, or
    could love the likes of me,
Far down into my bosom I have hid her
    words away—
Words she never meant, I reckon—but
    which cheer me on, to-day.

THE OTHER MAN'S BOY.

"If that there boy belonged to me," said
    Deacon Holliday,
"I'd hate to tell you what I'd do to make
    'im change his way.
I'd thrash 'im till he couldn't see; I'd
    chase 'im from the place!
There ain't no use of bein' mild or kind
    in such a case.
His father surely ought to know that he
    is doin' wrong
To spare the rod and let 'im go his own
    way right along—
Laws! If that boy was mine, I'll bet I'd
    make 'im change his way;
I'd lick 'im till he couldn't set!" said
    Deacon Holliday.

The Deacon had a little son who grew, as
    boys will grow,
And every boy must have his fun, or he's
    no boy, you know!
The outraged neighbors wondered why
    the Deacon was so mild,
They marveled that the father spared the
    rod and spoiled the child.
In every plot, however dark, that bad boy
    had a share;

And on two brows he left his mark in
    many a whitened hair!
Ah, the Deacon had a little son, who grew
    as boys will grow,
And the Deacon, when all's said and done,
    was just a man, you know!

WHEN THE RIFFLE IS MADE.

I s'pose I should feel like a man to-day fer
    the first time in my life,
Although I come purty nigh feelin' that
    way when Mollie was made my wife;
And that night when our little Albert was
    born, gol, didn't I sort of rise
Right up in my boots and feel as if I'd
    got about growed full size!
Still, they was somethin' I needed yit,
    and oh, it was far away!
But I buckled down and I worked fer it—
    and the farm is mine to-day!

When Mollie and me commenced, I guess
    I'd a hunderd dollars or so,
And she pitched in and she helped me
    save, but Moses! wasn't it slow!
Many and many a time I've gone and got
    blue and wanted to quit,
But Mollie'd say: "Keep a-goin', John,
    we'll make the riffle yit!"
That was afore little Albert come—when
    the Lord sent him, why then
'Course, no sich thought as givin' it up
    ever entered my head agen.

I've jist been up to the county seat—the
    last red cent is paid:

The farm belongs to me complete—the
    riffle at last is made,
And, oh, what a feelin' it is to know that
    the roof above your head
Belongs to you and has got to go to them
    you love, when you're dead!
No man has ever been quite a man who
    couldn't set down somewhere,
And say to himself: "This ground is
    mine and I've earned it fair and
    square."

Still, I ain't as happy by far, to-day, as
    I've often been before;
The last incumbrance is cleared away—
    but Mollie ain't here no more!
I promised I'd deed it over to her, but
    that can't never be,
For the Lord saw fit to take her away from
    little Albert and me,
And I'd give up all if she'd leave her
    grave, with her smiles and her patient
    ways,
To help me earn and to help me save, as
    in the old, happy days.

NATURE AND HER MOODS.

THE BIRTH OF THE ROSE.

A thistle once grew near a lily,
  A stately lily and fair,
And the wind swayed the one to the
    other,
  And the spirit of love was there.

And unto the lily and thistle
  A sweet little flower was born,
And the lily bent down to caress it,
  And her finger was pricked by a thorn.

The blood that the pale, pure lily,
  In the joy of her motherhood shed,
Gave the sweet little stranger its color,
  Gave the rose its beautiful red.

The rose that unto the lily
  And unto the thistle was born,
By the lily was given its beauty,
  By the thistle was given its thorn.

DAY AND NIGHT.

When it is day, and traffic roars about me
    in the street,
I need no guidance to elude the snares
    about my feet;
When it is day I go my way among the
    haunts of men,
Nor care who holds the stars in space, nor
    doubt nor question then;
I take the world for granted, and so toil
    and scheme away,
I hear the passing hour struck nor pray
    the hands might stay,
        When it is day.

When it is night, and I, alone, walk down
    the quiet lane
I hear the rustling blades of grass make
    God's high purpose plain;
When it is night the gleaming stars that
    through the distance roll
Send by the zephyrs messages to whisper
    to my soul,
I hear the chimes exult because of Time's
    unceasing flight
And feel my littleness, with all the
    Universe in sight,
        When it is night.

Life is day; the grave is night! Oh,
    when the pall is spread
Will there be constellations then still
    gleaming overhead?
When, after all the dreams and schemes
    that quicken men are gone,
When, after all the rush and roar the
    silent night comes on,
Will there be empty darkness and a pulse-
    less lump of clay,
Or will the Sun have just sent forth the
    first refulgent ray
        That wakes the day?

QUEER OLD NATURE.

"Why is it," asked a wondering child
   (Sweet, simple little thing),
"That the foolish tree puts on its clothes
   When the sun shines, in the spring,
And then, when chilly autumn comes
   And the winds of winter blow,
Why does it stand out there, all bare,
   In the frost and sleet and snow?"

"Wise Nature has arranged it thus,"
   I told the little one,
"The rustling leaves can only live
   Beneath a smiling sun;
The tree that, in the summer time,
   Makes shady bowers for you
Must have its rest, therefore it stands
   Asleep the winter through."

She sat in silence for a while
   And gazed far into space,
And lines of thought and trouble came
   To mar her childish face;
And so, at last, she turned and said:
   "I'm sorry for the tree,
And glad that Nature wasn't left
   To fix things up for me!"

APPLE BLOSSOMS.

The rose that blooms in the hot house
   Is rare and fair to see,
But still the fragrant blossoms
   Of the dear old apple tree
That stands in the edge of the orchard
   Somehow appeal to me!

I remember how she loved them
   And wore them on her breast;
Of all the flowers that bloomed, she liked
   The apple blossoms best,
And when we laid her away a bunch
   Of them in her hands was pressed!

The rose that blows in the hot-house
   Is rare and fair to see,
But the fragrance of the blossoms
   Of the dear, old apple tree
Somehow remains far sweeter
   And lovelier to me!

Or when 'tis joyous summer time
  Or when the wintry blast howls by—
Whate'er the land, whate'er the clime,
  'Tis all the same to me, for I
Find that the longest, dreariest day
When thou, my dear, art far away!

Or when the ground is white with snow
  And swallows to the South have flown,
Or when the rose and lily blow,
  Or fruit trees 'neath their burdens
    groan,
That day is shortest, sweetest, dear,
When thou, with thy glad smiles, art
    near!

FELLOWSHIP.

I sat upon the hillside yesterday
    And saw the fellowship that moved the
        herd;
I listened to a bell that, far away,
    Called striving men to hear the Savior's
        word,
And every bud there bursting whispered
        hope
To every blade upon the verdant slope.

I journeyed back into the noisy town,
    And mingled with the throng that
        choked the way:
I saw men push their weaker fellows
        down,
    And each man's watchword there was:
        "Will it pay?"
The bell of peace that I had heard before
Was silent in the turmoil and the roar.

THE WIND IN THE EVERGREENS.

When the drifted snow has hidden
    Roads and fences from the sight,
And the moon floats through the heavens
    Like a frozen thing, at night,
Flooding all the frigid stretches with a
        ghostly, bluish light,
I like to lie and conjure
    Up old half forgotten scenes,
As the savage wind goes howling
    Through the sighing evergreens.

There's a cottage I remember,
    With an orchard in the rear;
There's a winding pathway leading
    To a spring that bubbles near—
Ah, the dipper that I drank from bears
        the rust of many a year!—
There's a peach tree near the window
    Of the room where oft I lay
In the long ago, and listened
    To the wild wind howl away.

When a range of snowy mountains
    Stretch along the winding lane;
When the gently sloping meadow
    Has become an icy plain,
What a joy it is to snuggle under quilts
        and counterpane,

And hear the peach tree creaking,
  At the corner where it leans,
While the wind goes madly shrieking
  Through the mourning evergreens.

When the ruminating cattle
  Stand in bedding to their knees;
When the sheep are warmly sheltered,
  When the horses are at ease,
And the kittens in the kitchen are as
    happy as you please—
When father's work is ended,
  And mother sits and sews,
There's a wondrous mystic music
  In the angry wind that blows.

Ah, the rambling little sheepfold's
  Weatherbeaten, so they say;
The horses are no longer
  Munching at the fragrant hay—
Beneath the old-style kitchen stove no
    happy kittens play * * *
And, out behind the village church,
  A mossy gravestone leans
Above two mounds o'er which the wind
  Sighs through the evergreens.

BLOSSOMS AND FRUIT.

The bloom of the tree in the spring
Is a fragrant and beautiful thing,
    But, after all,
Is it half as sweet or as rare
As the fruit that is found hanging there
    In the fall?

A maiden's a beautiful thing—
A sweet, fresh blossom of spring—
    Careless and wild!
But rarest and fairest of all
Is she whose happy tears fall
    On her first-born child!

THE CRICKET.

I hear the cricket grinding out his oft
  repeated lay,
And know the time for leaves to fall is not
  so far away;
It is a plaintive song he sings and always
  just the same,
But Nature fixed it so for him, and he is
  not to blame.

Ah, what a wondrous set of lungs it is
  that he employs!
There's such a little bit of him and such a
  lot of noise,
Wherefore this insect brings to mind some
  men who seem to take
The view that men are measured by the
  noise that they can make.

THE PAINTED LEAVES.

CHILD.

All the trees are gold and crimson and
　　they look like pictures now;
Did the one who spread the colors do it
　　with a brush, or how?
All the big Outdoors is painted, there is
　　color everywhere,
But I didn't see the artist when he came
　　and put it there.

ANSWER.

There's an ancient faithful painter, and a
　　magic brush he wields;
'Tis his work you see when looking at the
　　woods across the fields;
Oh, he uses splendid colors, and he shows
　　unequaled skill,
But no child has ever seen him, and no
　　maiden ever will.

CHILD.

Does he bring his pretty colors in the
　　night when I'm in bed?
Tell me how he paints the treetops, up so
　　high above his head?

Does he climb a long, long ladder that
  goes half-way to the sky—
What if he should ever tumble when he's
  working up so high!

ANSWER.

Yes, when you are sweetly dreaming this
  old artist works away,
And while you, awake, are playing, he
  keeps toiling on all day;
But he needs no lengthy ladder, so put off
  your idle fear,
He will never fall or fail us in his autumn
  painting, dear.

CHILD.

All the leaves are gold and crimson; what
  an artist he must be!
And how swiftly he must labor to get
  over every tree!
But I wish he came in springtime; it's a
  pity, after all,
That he makes the leaves so pretty just
  before they have to fall!

OCTOBER DAYS.

The squirrels are barking in the trees
    And the leaves unto crimson are
      turning,
And the smell of wood smoke floats along
    on the breeze
    From the brush heaps the farmer is
      burning.

The song-birds are singing their plaintive
    farewells
    To the brooks that are silently flowing,
And over the hills comes the tinkling of
    bells
    And the echoes of nutters halloing.

A sigh for the days that are lost in the
    past,
    When a bare-footed boy did his dream-
      ing,
When the world spread around him, com-
    placent and vast,
And his heart never ached after profitless
    scheming.

NATURE'S FUNERAL DAY.

O, Indian summer days,
When the hills are blue with haze,
And the sounds of tinkling cow-bells come
    afar across the lea,
What a sense of rest there lies
In the azure of the skies,
And what peace there is reflected from
    the bosom of the sea.

In a holy calm the year
Is about to disappear,
Merely merging with the past in solemn,
    sweet solemnity!
And I, too, would linger till
The blue haze is on the hill—
Serene in Indian summer, when the sum-
    mons comes to me.

THE WIND AND THE LEAVES.

The wind is fate,
  The leaves are men—
They are blown along for a little space,
  And then
A few emerge and tumble ahead,
  Over and over and over again,
In a maddening race,
  And here and there
One lodges and clings in a lonesome place,
Until, at last, but a single leaf
  Whirls onward into the far Somewhere.

And the many leaf-men that are left
    behind
  Gather in clusters here and there
And are whirled about by the wilful wind,
  And, at last, when the great white quilt
    is spread,
And all is over and done
  They silently lie and slowly rot,
  Each on the barren little spot
Where its troubles were begun.

THE DYING YEAR.

I have no tear for the dying year,
   No wreath of vain regret
To place with those upon the bier
   That the world will soon forget—
Let hopeless others turn and gaze
   Back on the fading past,
And sigh again for blissful days
   That were too sweet to last—
I have no tear for the dying year
   That the world will soon forget.

I have no tear for the dying year,
   No sigh for yesterday;
The spreading future stretches clear,
   And Hope still points the way!
Let him for whom the sun has set
   Bemoan the fading past;
To him a wreath of vain regret
   For days too sweet to last—
I have no tear for the dying year,
   Since Hope still points the way.

MISCELLANEOUS VERSES.

THE THINGS THAT ARE DENIED.

Why must I ever tell him "No"—
  My pleading baby boy?
The things he craves 'twould please me so
  To witness him enjoy.
Poor child, he leaves me with a sigh
  And doubting in his mind,
Because he does not know that I
  Am "cruel to be kind."

I long for things I cannot get;
  In vain I toil away;
And oft I doubt and grieve and fret
  As he has done to-day.
Why am I thus denied? Why do
  I seek and fail to find?
Mayhap my loving Father, too,
  Is "cruel to be kind."

THE OLD GRIND.

Sometimes I look upon the rich
  With envy in my breast,
And think how pleasant it would be
  To just "saw off" and rest—
To smoke cigars and loaf around,
  While others worked away—
With plenty "salted down," of course,
  For the future rainy day.

Oh what a joy 'twould be to tell
  The man who bosses me
That I was tired of his style—
  To brace up and be free!
And, in the lazy mornings, how
  I'd like to lie abed,
And what a pleasure to get out
  And be a thoroughbred!

Such thoughts I have sometimes, but
    when
  I'm ill and have to stay
Indoors a day or two, ah, then
  My envy fades away!
I think of all the boys at work,
  And know no peace of mind,
Until they let me out and I
  Resume the good old grind!

A HAPPY MAN.

I have no lofty station,
  Nor riches nor renown—
An atom in creation,
  I travel up and down—
I come and go unheeded,
  I toil as millions do,
But O, I still am needed,
  And gladness claims me, too!
The sky is blue above me,
  And Hope points out the way—
You tell me that you love me,
  And you are three to-day.

I envy not my neighbor
  Whose name is known to men;
He may not need to labor
  With scythe or pick or pen,
But yet, despite his riches,
  He still is poor, for he
Has not the sweet care which is
  Confided unto me!
Blue, blue the sky above me
  While Hope points out the way
And you are here to love me,
  You who are three to-day!

THE WAYS.

Do you traverse a way
  That is likely to end
At Something, some day,
  My friend?

Or, do you belong
To the great plodding throng
  On the broad, level way
That leads to Nowhere—
  That will end, some day,
In Nothing, out there?

There are paths leading out
  From this broad, level way—
You have seen them, no doubt,
  For you pass them each day—
That lead to Somewhere,
  That glorious place,
So distant, so fair—
  Like a mirage in space!

But these pathways, you say,
  Are so stony and steep!
And the broad, level way
  Is so easy to keep!
You have heard of Somewhere,
And you'd like to go there
  If a way could be found

That was easy, and wound
  In a smooth, broad course that led on
    around
And up the height,
Where the city stands, a glorious sight,
Peopled by only immortals, and where
There is honor for each that, at last, gets
    there!

Ah, there is no way that is level and broad
  Leading up to this glorious place, Some-
    where,
And no man yet who has only trod
A way that is easy and smooth and broad
Has ever succeeded in getting there!

A TRANSFORMATION.

Ere you went to live upon "The Avenue"
  You were sweet and fair and jovial
    with me;
But a sudden change has taken place in
    you,
Since you've gone to live upon "The
    Avenue,"
  And my maid, so fair and free,
  Where, oh haughty one, is she,
Since you've gone to live upon "The
    Avenue?"

Since you've gone to live upon "The
    Avenue"
  You are distant, you are stiff, and you
    are cold;
You have donned the ugly false and put
    off the lovely true,
Since you've gone to live upon "The
    Avenue,"
  And my jolly maid of old
  Kneels before a calf of gold,
Since you've gone to live upon "The
    Avenue."

THE MAN WHO FAILED.

"With you," he cried, "to cheer me on
   I'll brush all obstacles away,
And scale the heights whereon is fame,
And all the world shall praise thy name
   And envy you, some day."

Ah, that was many a year ago!
   He hasn't scaled the height.
But if—oh heaven!—if he were
Not sorely handicapped by her,
   He often thinks he might.

THE MEETING

One day, in Paradise,
  Two angels, beaming, strolled
Along the amber walk that lies
  Beside the street of gold.

At last they met and gazed
  Into each other's eyes,
Then dropped their harps, amazed,
  And stood in mute surprise.

And other angels came,
  And, as they lingered near,
Heard both at once exclaim;
  "Say, how did you get here?"

THE ANSWER.

The great man knelt in prayer:
"O, Lord of Hosts," he said,
"Permit thy blessing now to rest
    Upon thy servant's head!—
Men gnash their teeth and scowl at me,
O, give them eyes, that they may see!

"My wordly store is great, O, Lord;
    My power increases day by day;
Here I bestow, as Thou dost know,
    If there I take away—
Yet men cry out, reviling me,
Lord, give them eyes, that they may see!

"Upon thy footstool, Lord, behold
    A hundred spires rise!
Through them thy servant points the way
    To glories in the skies—
Still, men stand here reviling me,
O, give them eyes, that they may see!"

Unto the great man kneeling there
    A Thunderous Voice replied:
"Thy worldly store indeed is great,
    Thy power vast and wide—
But who, thou worm, has given to thee
Authority to act for Me?

93

"I see the traces of thy hand!
   A starving child is there,
  Deep in the shadow of the spire
   That thou hast reared in air!—
  Speak out, thou worm! Who vested thee
  With power to rearrange for Me?

"Here thou hast taken ten away,
   There thou hast given one—
  Who fixed the toll to be retained
   For this that thou hast done?
  Speak out! Speak out! Who vested thee
  With rights to give and take for Me?"

INNOCENCE.

She took a fragile flower from a bunch
    against her breast—
  Sweet little maiden that she was!
Its petals for a moment at her honeyed
    lips were pressed—
  Dainty little maiden that she was!
Then she bade me sweet "Good day,"
Threw the scented bud away—
And I watched it where it lay—
  Pretty little maiden that she was!

I knelt beside the flower where it fell upon
    the floor—
  Tender little maiden that she was!
I fondly pressed it to my lips, as she had
    done before—
  Darling little maiden that she was!
And then, turning suddenly,
At the corner I could see
Her slyly watching me—
  Cunning little maiden that she was!

TEARS AND SMILES.

The skies cannot always be clear,
    My dear;
The merriest eye must still have its tear,
    My dear;
The clouds that are frowning above us
    to-day
Will presently break and go floating away,
And the skies will be blue that are sullen
    and gray,
      My dear!

We can't have just happiness here,
    My dear;
You would never be glad if you ne'er shed
    a tear,
      My dear;
The sorrow that lurks in your bosom
    to-day,
Like the clouds, when you've wept, will
    go floating away,
And the skies will be blue that are sullen
    and gray,
      My dear!

If it's going to rain, it will rain,
    My dear;
No matter how bitterly we may complain,
    My dear;

There are sorrows that every good woman
    must bear;
There are griefs in which every good man
    has a share;
It is only the fool who has never a care,
      My dear!

The skies cannot always be clear,
      My dear;
Sweets wouldn't be sweet were no bitter-
    ness here,
      My dear;
There could never be joy if there never
    was sorrow,
The sobs of to-day are the smiles of
    to-morrow,
And there's gladness as well as vain
    trouble to borrow,
      My dear!

THE ONE BELOW.

I gazed on piles of marble—
  Saw servants come and go,
And my breast was filled with envy,
  And my soul was steeped in woe.

* * *

It was a tired cripple who stopped me at
    the gate,
And Hope, I saw, was his, although his
    burden was so great;
And, as I bought his pencils, I saw his
    thankful smile,
And envy turned to pity, and I bade him
    stay awhile.

"And do you, brother, never," I said,
    "bewail your lot?
And do you never envy men who have
    what you have not?
Is life still worth the effort, and can you,
    brother, too,
Still thank your God for favors that he
    has bestowed on you?"

He smiled, and then he answered:
    "There stands in yonder square
A blind man who is begging of the people
    passing there:

He cannot see their faces; but there, day
    after day,
He, pleading, stands, with outstretched
    hands, to those that pass his way.

"I see the blue of Heaven; I see the
    glorious sun;
I see the world, and marvel at the things
    that God has done;
And when the day is ended I leave the
    market place,
And hold my baby in my arms and look
    upon her face!

"Sometimes I feel the burden and bend
    beneath its weight;
Sometimes I cry aloud against the cruel-
    ties of Fate—
But there he stands, with outstretched
    hands, before his fellow-men;
I gaze into his sightless eyes, and I am
    glad again!"

* * *

He hobbled on. I watched him
    With painful steps depart;
He took my pennies with him,
    And left a buoyant heart.

THE SWEET OLD WAY.

We live, alas, in an age of greed,
  Greed of power and greed of gain—
Gold begins and ends our creed,
  We weigh the purse instead of the
    brain!
Chivalry's buried, never again
  To be resurrected, so they say—
But, in spite of the struggle for riches, men
  Still fall in love in the sweet old way.

The days when honor was all are dead;
  We have little time for rhyme or art;
The world of to-day obeys the head,
  We have turned in rebellion against the
    heart;
But through the rush and the strife and
    the roar,
  Still come the sounds of gentle sighs,
And men are thrilled as they were of yore
  By the looks of love in women's eyes!

Fame is no longer for him alone
  That wins in the field or charms with
    his pen;
By the lengths of their bank accounts are
    known
  The grades of our modern gentlemen;

Few of us even have time to pray
    To the God that is still enthroned
      above—
But women still charm in the sweet, old
    way,
    And money-mad men still fall in love.

THE MAN WHO IS NOT NEEDED.

I'm sixty years of age to-day,
  And I have worked and slaved,
And someone else shall presently
  Get all that I have saved!
    But it is not
    The simple thought
Of going that I deplore;
    'Tis this: When I
    In the cold earth lie,
They'll think of me no more!

I've labored on from day to day
  With one hope in my mind,
'Twas that when I was laid away
  I'd leave a void behind—
    Something, you know,
    To always show
That I had lived and wrought;
    But now, at last,
    That dream is past—
I've got to share the common lot.

I've thrown a fever off to-day
  And risen from my bed;
For months I've been but helpless clay,
  With wild thoughts in my head.
    I'd fondly thought
    The mill would not

Run if I were not there to see—
　　But it kept right on
　　While I was gone,
And that's the thing that saddens me.

THE BANISHED VISION.

I saw a splendid castle whose towers cleft
    the air,
And troops of hurrying servants spoke in
    frightened whispers there;
Beside a bed all richly spread the kneeling
    master wept,
And, pressed against its mother's breast,
    a fragile infant slept.

Outside the castle gates I saw a ghostly
    rider sit
Upon a pale, impatient steed that madly
    champed its bit,
And, as I looked, the gates were swung to
    let the rider through,
And then a baby's laughter swept the
    castle from my view.

I turned and kissed a rosy cheek and
    stroked a curly head,
And pitied him who knelt beside that
    richly-covered bed;
I heard a happy mother's song, and,
    hearing, was aware
That gladness may be far away from
    towers that cleave the air.

THE INFIDEL.

O man of eloquent speech,
  O man of massive brain.
What is this thing you preach,
  And what do your followers gain?
You have seen the stars in the sky,
  You have watched the billows roll,
You have heard the infant cry,
You have heard the mother sigh,
And still you have flowery words to deny
  The existence of the soul!

You have searched the Bible through,
  O man of wonderful brain,
And you hold its fallacies up to view,
  But what do your followers gain?
You have garnered a wealth of lore,
  And you splendidly deal it out,
From your lips the flowery sentences pour,
And men who had simple faith before
  Depart with sickening doubt.

But I have knelt at a knee,
  O man of wonderful scope,
And one with a soul has given to me
  The trust that fosters hope!
And the simple faith she had to give
  Will live a thousand years for each

THE INFIDEL.

Brief year, O man, that you may live,
 To charm with your flowery speech.
O, man of words that burn,
 O man of words that sway,
What do you offer in return
 For the faith you would take away?
The trust she gave was free,
 O man of wonderful brain—
You would destroy for pelf, but she
 Taught not for selfish gain!
You have garnered a wealth of lore,
 She was moved by a Mind above;
You pile up a wordly store—
 She gave from the fountain of love!

You have searched the Good Book through,
 O man of massive brain,
You hold its fallacies up to view—
 You garner gold and you scatter pain!
But I have knelt at a knee,
 And I have listened to you,
And her prayers come back, and I know
   that she
 Who loved me and taught me knew—
That the word she gave to me
 Is the wonderful word that is true.

HER TEARS.

Let others bask in her smiles!
      I know
That her yearning heart is mine,
      Although
    She pretends to be gay
    With another, to-day—
Last night I caused her tears to flow!

She is making a fool of him!
      I know
'Tis not his love sets her cheeks
      Aglow!
    Let him bask in her smiles,
    And be fooled by her wiles—
Last night I caused her tears to flow!

Oh, dearer than all her smiles
      May be
Is the glorious charm of knowing
      That she
    Who pretends to be gay
    With another, to-day,
Wept, last night, when she quarreled with
    me!

WORDS IN THE SAND.

They strolled together on the shore
    He held her little hand,
And where the waves had dashed before
    They wrote words in the sand.

They wrote the words that lovers say,
    They joined their names together,
And merry-hearted took away
    No thoughts of stormy weather.

The waves of Time have broken o'er
    Her heart and his since then,
As the waves have washed the sandy shore
    And left it bare again.

And the words they fashioned in the sand
    Are gone and gone forever,
For the heart is but a shifting strand,
    Wave-washed—and constant never.

HIS NEW SUIT.

I remember well the way
She looked up at me that day
When I first put on the gray,
   And said good-bye, back there in '63.
She and I were sweethearts then,
And I hear her voice again,
   As she nestled up to me,
Saying in her gentle way:
"Ah, how brave you look in gray,
And how tall and handsome, too,
Gray's the color, dear, for you!"

There's a ragged suit of gray
She has long had laid away—
   There are memories that cling around
     it, too;
But the years have come and gone,
And at present I have on
   A suit of Uncle Sam's beloved blue.

When she saw me yesterday
She wiped a tear away
For the memory of the gray—
   That dear, old, ragged suit of '63,
And she sweetly spoke again—
Spoke more fervently than then
   As she nestled up to me,

Saying, in her gentle way:
"Ah, how brave you looked in gray!
But you're braver still in blue,
Blue's the color, dear, for you!"

VISIONS OF THE PAST.

THE WEARY ONE.

The good old days—the good old days—
    ah! life was sweeter then
Than it is since I must share the cares
    that weigh on toiling men.
The fruit that grew on the bending trees
    when I was young and free
Seemed sweeter far and juicier than fruit
    now seems to me.
Oh, for another happy day back there in
    the long ago,
Perched in the dear old cherry tree, and
    swinging to and fro!
And oh for the big red cherries that I ate
    with a relish then,
For the cherries are all wormy since I
    share the cares of men!

THE SAGE.

Ah! the good old days would cease to
    charm if, with your present tastes,
You were back again on the lonesome
    farm, with its briers and stony wastes.
And you didn't enjoy the good old days
    when you had them to enjoy,

And you wouldn't now if you might again
    be a freckle-featured boy!
You think that the fruit was juicier then
    and sweeter than 'tis to-day;
But fruit still grows upon the trees in the
    same old-fashioned way.
And you found no worms in your cherries
    then, but 'tis certain that they were
    there;
You weren't looking for worms when you
    were a boy, and didn't care!

WHERE SHE IS.

I do not mind the rabble in the street,
  The never-ceasing conflict and the whir;
Around me clatter many tired feet,
  But dreamily I listen unto her.

She hums a little song and I can hear
  Cool brooklets flowing gently to the sea;
She smiles, and blossom-laden trees appear
  In fancy's dreamy vistas unto me.

What matter, if the town be hot and dry?
  Where she is, fragrant flowers ever
    blow;
The noise and conflict still go on, but I
  Forget and dream of moments long ago,
And gleaming sails, that drifted slowly by.

GOING WITH THE CROWD.

Like a ship without a rudder
  That goes drifting here and there,
Idly tossing, weather beaten,
  Never getting anywhere—
Veering with the daily changes of the tide,
On the wave or in the trough, upon her
      side—
Is the man who merely shuffles
  With the crowd along the way,
Bringing up to-morrow evening
  Where he started yesterday.

Better far a wooden dory
  With a purpose that is plain
Than a stately liner tossing
  Rudderless upon the main!
Better far to toil obscurely for a time
On some rocky path no other dares to
      climb
Than carelessly to shuffle
  With the crowd along the way,
Bringing up to-morrow evening
  Where you started yesterday.

I greet the man who bravely
  Takes a course and fares along—
Turns his steps into some rugged
  Path untrodden by the throng;

GOING WITH THE CROWD.

Fame is deftly interlacing laurels now
To be wreathed upon the lonely toiler's
        brow—
Leaves that never come through drifting
    With the crowd along the way,
Bringing up to-morrow evening
    Where you started yesterday!

THE COURSE OF LOVE.

'Twas midnight, and the silvery moon
  Beamed down upon the scene
Where Harold planned to carry off
  The lovely Geraldine.
He was a brave and handsome lad,
  She was as sweet as fair,
But, oh, her heavy-fisted dad
  Opposed the loving pair.

He came out from behind a tree—
  He gave the cuckoo's call,
And waited for the lovely maid
  Who held his heart in thrall.
Eftsoons she softly raised the sash,
  And whispered: "I am here";
He ceased to gnaw his young mustache,
  And cried: "Hist! Hist! my dear!"

She "histed" once; she "histed" twice,
  Her father snored away;
The lover dragged his ladder up,
  And brought it into play;
He stood upon the lowest round,
  While she leaned out above—
The moon was happy to have found
  This blissful scene of love.

"And are you sure," the maiden cried,
  "That you will ever be

As brave and true as you are now,
   And always cherish me?''
''As long,'' the lover made reply,
   ''As yonder moon doth shine
And take her course across the sky,
   I'll love you, my divine!''

He took another upward step,
   Her heart began to quake;
''Oh, what,'' she thought, ''would happen
     now
   If father should awake?''
Up, up, the happy lover crept
   Till she could feel his breath,
And still the cruel father slept,
   And all was still as death.

Another step, another round,
   And then their lips would meet—
Alas! the ladder broke, and he
   Fell twenty-seven feet!
The clatter would have raised the dead,
   It raised her sleeping sire,
Who quickly bounded out of bed,
   Nor sought to curb his ire.

They found the lover lying low,
   His clothes were badly torn;
He'd fallen in a bramble-bush,
   And met with many a thorn.
At last they brought him round again,
   Her father bade him go,
He didn't stop to argue then,
   And it was better so!

Ah, that was many years ago,
   They're married, he and she,
But each unto another, and
   As happy as can be.
She has a son that she's afraid
   May throw himself away—
And he's the father of a maid
   He watches well, to-day!

IF.

When all is over,
   And the dear one lies
Under the cover
Of blossoms and clover—
   When the kind, weary eyes
   Are sightless forever—
How thick and how vast do the ugly
   "if's" rise!
"If I had been kinder—if I had obeyed,
  The hand of the reaper, mayhap, had
    been stayed!
O, if I had thought, O, if I had cared,
  What heart-breaking sorrows might she
    have been spared!"

   O, happy the lover,
    Thrice happy the son,
  If, when all is over
    And the dear, patient one
  Lies under the cover
    Of blossoms and clover,
No "ifs" come trooping to taunt and
    torment!
  O happy his lot
  Who can say: "I would not
  Undo or change aught—"
Who requited her love ere she went!

IF.

When all is over
   And the dear one lies
Under the cover
Of blossoms and clover,
   When the kind, weary eyes
Are sightless forever,
O would that there never
   Were "ifs" to arise!

MISS "I-DON'T-CARE."

She is sweet, petite, and witty,
    But, alas, she's heartless, too!
If you know her, oh, I pity—
    From my soul I pity you!
Half a hundred hearts are breaking
    For this maid, so sweet, so fair—
She with merriment is shaking,
    And exclaiming, "I don't care!"

"Maiden," cried I once, "I love you;
    Let me claim your heart as mine;
Every star that is above you
    But for you would cease to shine!"
"Ah, you foolish, foolish fellow,
    Why bore me with this affair?"
She replied, in accents mellow,
    "Let the stars fall, I don't care!"

"But my heart is fiercely burning!
    I must win your love!" I cried;
Smiling cruelly, and turning
    Half away, the maid replied:
"Ah, your breast is all on fire!
    That is awful, I declare!
Still, if you will build a pyre
    In your bosom I don't care!"

Fifty times I've knelt before her
    And in many ways I've sought

To invoke a love spell o'er her,
  But it all has come to naught!
Yesterday I swore I'd die if
  She my fortune would not share—
"Die then," said she, with a sigh, "if
  That will help you—I don't care!"

HAPPINESS.

"I would be happy," Greed's slave cries,
  "Could I but learn some way
To win the great, elusive prize
  That ever flees from me—
  I would be happy could I be
  A millionaire to-day."

"I would be happy," Youth cries out
  "If Fate would grant me fame!
O, that I might hear people shout
  My praises as I passed along—
  O, that in story and in song
  I might embalm my name!"

Behold where happiness is found:
  Beneath yon spreading tree
A fool, half stretched upon the ground,
  Holds in his teeth a bit of clay
  And blows white rings of smoke
    away—
  From sad ambition free.

THE MAN OF FAITH.

He is the bravest man
  Who has the faith to feel
That God's above to guide
  Him on through woe or weal—
To him who has no doubt
  How can there come a fear?
He plunges in or rushes out,
  Believing God is near,
And, though by dangers hedged about
  Pursueth his career,
For where there lurketh doubt,
  There, only, can be fear.

He is the strongest man
  Who has the faith sublime
To feel that he is kept
  In God's view all the time;
He calmly goes his way,
  When once that way is plain,
And keeps ascending day by day
  The height he is to gain;
The part that God gave him to play
  He plays with might and main,
And never wanders from the way,
  Since God has made it plain.

O, for the faith that lifts
  Men over earth's affairs—

The faith that strengthens hearts
  And blots out human cares!
To him who has no doubt
  How can there come a fear?
He plunges in or rushes out,
  Believing God is near.
And, though by dangers hedged about,
  Pursueth his career,
For where there lurketh doubt,
  There, only, can be fear.

LIVING IT OVER.

"If I had my life to live over,
    And could know what I know to-day;
        If I could go back
        O'er the uneven track,
    I would travel a different way.
    The prospect beyond me is gloomy,
        My pathway is rocky and steep;
        I must toil, though I know
        That the crops which I sow
    Are only for others to reap!
    Alas for the years that I've squandered,
        And the chances I've frittered away!
    Would that I might live it all over,
        Knowing life as I know it to-day!"

"And if it were all to live over,
    If you knew all you know to-day,
        If you could go back
        O'er the uneven track,
    You would still sing your pitiful lay,
    For the man who sits idle, regretting
        The chances that lie in the past
        Is never the one
        Whose work is well done,
    However his fortunes are cast!
    There's a use for the years that are
        squandered

And the chances men fritter away;
The man who succeeds is the man who
    can build
On the failures of yesterday.''

THE QUARREL.

"There are quite as good fish
    In the sea
As anyone ever has caught,"
    said he.

"But few of the fish—
    In the sea
Will bite at such bait as you've got,"
    Said she.

To-day he is gray and his line's put away,
    But he often looks back with regret;
She's still "in the sea," and how happy
        she'd be
    If he were a fisherman yet!

THE MAN WHO DIDN'T RISE.

He worked away
From day to day
Year in, year out, he came and went;
  And others passed him in the race
  And lines began to mark his face,
And in his breast was discontent.

  "I wonder why,"
    He moaned, "that I
Am stranded here, as on a rock?
  While others rise I'm doomed to stay!"
  And, ever as he worked away,
He kept one eye upon the clock.

LOVE'S MIRROR.

I.

The sky was draped with somber clouds,
  A chill was in the air;
My love was cold and gloominess
  Extended everywhere.

I mingled with the busy throng,
  And scanned the faces there;
Each seemed a living mirror of
  Bereavement or despair.

II.

My loved one smiled upon me and
  The world was bright again;
E'en though the wind blew from the north
  It did not chill me then.

Again I mingled with the throng,
  And saw but gladness when
I peered into the faces of
  Those erst unhappy men.

CONTENTMENT.

The man who grinds me down and thrives
    upon my daily toil
Owns acres by the thousand, while I've
    not a foot of soil;
And in his vaults 'tis said that he has
    millions stored away,
While I must labor for the things I need
    from day to day,
Yet I would not change places with this
    multi-millionaire,
For I have peace of mind, while he is
    weighted down with care!

I have a wife and little ones, who fill my
    foolish heart,
While he, in crusty loneliness, is doomed
    to live apart!
He never felt two little arms around his
    wrinkled neck;
He is not loved, although his gold is
    measured by the peck;
He cannot go to bed at night and slumber
    as I can—
No, no! I would not, if I could, change
    places with this man!

And when the labor of the day is done
    and I repair

Unto my humble home, to eat the dinner
 steaming there,
Ah, what a joy awaits me then! What
 prince's appetite
Could ever be compared to that which I
 have every night?
But, as for him—the millionaire—he
 lunches on a crust,
Because dyspepsia mocks at him, and tells
 him that he must!

Oh, let this sallow, wrinkled man grind on
 and save and save,
And I will be content to keep on toiling
 as a slave;
Oh, let him have his sleepless nights, while
 happy dreams are mine;
Oh, let him be the upas tree that holds no
 clinging vine!
Though he has wealth that lifts him high
 in thoughtless people's sight,
I'll never envy him while I can soundly
 sleep at night.

LINES TO A COBBLER.

Men look upon him with disdain,
  And scout his humble trade;
Poor soul, he has no teeming brain,
  No learning to parade!
He only sits, from day to day,
  And plies his awl and thread;
No tender fancies ever play
  'Round that dull, grizzled head.

Still, be not hasty to despise
  This man of humble parts,
For, though he has not drawn a prize,
  In choosing of the arts,
His awl obeys a master's hand,
  And, oh, to be supreme
In any honest thing is grand
  Beyond the poet's dream!

LOST CANDOR.

I used to hold her on my knees,
  And softly stroke her sunny curls;
I used to pat her dimpled cheeks,
  And call her loveliest of girls;
She used to look into my eyes,
  And smile and nestle down, serene—
But that was when the maid was four,
  And I had just turned seventeen.

I met her yesterday again,
  She placed a little hand in mine;
She looked into my eyes and then
  I saw a blush that was divine!
I thought of those old days when we
  Had romped around upon the green—
When she was four and frank and free,
  And I had just turned seventeen.

Ah, would that I might speak to her
  As freely as I did of yore;
Would that she were as frank with me
  As when she was a child of four!
But words that I would say to-day
  Unto this graceful little queen
Forsake me, since I'm thirty-one
  And she is stately and eighteen.

THE LITTLE OLD CHURCH
DOWN TOWN.

Down in the smoke, where the roar and
    the rush
    Of traffic is heard all day;
Where the cars and the trucks and the
    carriages crush
    The cripple that gets in the way;
Surrounded by buildings that tower above
    And flanked by a bright bit of sod—
An oasis left there in the desert of trade—
    Is a spot that belongs to God.

I steal through the half-open door and sit
    down
    In an old-fashioned pew to dream—
To forget the roar of the money-mad
    town—
    And through a memorial window a
    beam
Of God's sweet sunlight forces itself,
    And illumines the dark old place;
And a smile of sweet welcome seems to
    spread
    O'er the pictured Saviour's face.

And so for a while my mind is free
    From the world and its mad affairs,

Again my mother sits next to me,
  And I hear her whispered prayers!
O, blissful hour! O, sacred spot,
  What sweet old memories do ye bring!
O, cramped and crowded house of God,
  What glories still around thee cling!

Again I can hear the sweet old chimes,
  As I slowly move away,
And I'm better for thinking of those old
    times—
  I've communed with Him to-day!
Surrounded by buildings that tower
    above,
  And flanked by a bit of sod,
There is rest, there is hope, there is happi-
    ness
  On this spot that belongs to God.

SINCE SHE'S AWAY.

She's gone away—
  The sky is blue,
But it was bluer yesterday;
  The breeze, I trow, was sweeter, too,
Before she went away.

She's gone away—
  There seems to be
A lack of something here, to-day;
  The town is dead and drear to me
Since she has gone away.

She's gone away—
  I never knew,
Until she started, yesterday,
  How fair she was, how helpful, too—
And she is far—so far away!

She's gone away—
  I would that she
Were coming back again, to-day,
  For it has just occurred to me
How dear she is, since she's away!

ON LIFE'S LADDER.

I.

For him who seeks to rise few hands reach
    down to claim his grip,
Few warning words are heard above to
    save him from a slip;
Each upward step he takes must be
    through efforts of his own,
For everyone that's gained the top would
    like to be alone!

II.

For him who stumbles on the way a
    thousand hands reach out
To grasp and pull him down into the
    misery-haunted rout!
There's scanty welcome at the top for him
    that wins, but oh
What joyous greetings does he get who
    joins the ranks below!

A WISH.

If some good fairy were to come
    To me to-day and say:
"One wish I have to grant to thee—
    One wish, come say, what shall it be?
    And have it while you may,"

Dost think that I would ask for wealth,
    Or for unbounded fame?
Nay, riches would not charm me then,
Nor power to wield a glorious pen
    Would be the boon I'd claim.

But I would make this simple wish:
    That I might once more stand
Back in the happy days of old,
With faith in the rainbow's pot of gold
    And glad belief in fairy land!

PASSING OF A GOOD SAMARITAN.

Lay him away,
 It matters not where;
Dig a hole in the ground,
 And deposit him there;
'Twill be useless to raise
 A shaft o'er his head,
For Heaven's aware
 Of the fact that he's dead!

Lowly his lot,
 And humble his sphere;
The world—the big, busy world knew not
 That he ever was sent to minister here;
He gathered no millions, he built up no
  trusts,—
 He cornered no markets, robbed no one
  of bread;
His raiment was ragged, he lived upon
  crusts—
 But Heaven's aware of the fact that
  he's dead!

Did he worship in church
 In the orthodox way?
Did the rafters ring when
 It was his turn to pray?
Alas, I know not—
 But let it be said

That Heaven's aware
　Of the fact that he's dead!

The orphan he fanned
　Through feverish days
May live or may not
　To cherish his praise;
The sick that he nourished when stricken
　　himself,
　The starving that, when he was hungry,
　　he fed
May pray for him now, or may not, as
　　they list—
　But Heaven's aware of the fact that
　　he's dead!

Lay him away,
　It matters not where;
Dig a hole in the earth,
　And deposit him there;
When the last trumpet sounds
　He will hear, he will hear
As well as the man
　O'er whose head people rear
The highest of columns—
　Aye, put him to bed!
If there is a God He will not forget
　That this lowly man lived—and is dead!

A man who had delved in the lore of the
    ages
  And could tell you the weight of the
    stars,
Who had added wise words unto Science's
    pages
  And written an essay on Mars,
Arrived at the startling conclusion, one
    day,
That lawyers who plead and preachers
    who pray,
  And doctors who claim to subdue peo-
    ple's ills
  With scalpels and nostrums and poison-
    ous pills
Were nothing but swindlers, each in his
    way.

But the man who had delved in the lore
    of the ages
  And studied the far-away stars,
Who had earned the proud right to be
    classed with the sages,
  One day got in front of the cars!
They picked him up tenderly; put him to
    bed,
And, as he lay groaning and moaning,
    half-dead,

A preacher came in and knelt down at
  his side
And called on the God that the sage
  had denied,
And he heartily joined in the prayers that
  were said.

Yet the man who had delved in the lore of
  the ages,
And could name all the stars in the sky,
Who had added wise words unto Science's
  pages,
  Was not quite ready to die!
He summoned a surgeon and patiently lay
While the "brute of a butcher" was saw-
  ing away:
  He took all the poisons they gave him
  to take,
  Forgetting that "doctoring's only a
  fake"—
And arose and hobbled away, one day.

Now the man who has delved in the lore
  of the ages
And can tell you the names of the stars,
Who has earned the proud right to be
  classed with the sages
  And was knocked galley west by the
  cars—
Who prayed when he thought he was go-
  ing to die,
Who, ill, sent for him of whom, well, he
  fought shy,
  Has hired a lawyer to take up his case—
  To sue for the damages done to his face
And the leg that he lost when the train
  went by.

THE MAN WHO WAS FORGOTTEN.

"Set him there, where he may see me;
    Let me hold his little hand;
Keep my memory before him
    So that he may understand.
Let him look upon my visage
    As I draw my latest breath;
Let him close my eyes, when, sightless,
    They shall stare at him, in death.

"Let him look; he may remember!
    In the years to come, perchance
He may still recall his father,
    Back across the dim expanse.
God, thou hast been kind—I thank
        Thee!
    Thou hast given me to see
Him whose flesh is mine—I pray Thee
    Let my son remember me."

The wondering child bent over,
    And he kissed his father's brow;
They that listened heard the grating
    Of the sable boatman's prow;
There were tears and sobs and sighing,
    But the father only smiled,
And, in death, still gazed up fondly
    At the prattling little child.

ENVOY.

There's a gravestone that is mossy, and a
    name is carved thereon;
There's a wife that once was widowed,
    but the years have come and gone;
There's a son to whom a father's tender
    love is all unknown,
And the name he bears is not the name
    that's carved upon the stone!

A SONG FOR THE SELFISH.

When you and I were young, my dear,
   Ere lines had marked your brow,
Ere God had sent the loved ones here
   That cling about us now—
When you and I were free from care,
We thought the world was very fair—
   When you and I were young, my dear.

But we are older now, my dear,
   And worried by the cares
Of those who cling around us here
   And have their love affairs—
Ere you were grieved by others' woes
You were as radiant as a rose,
   But now your brow has furrows, dear.

When you and I were young, my dear,
   We thought the Lord was good,
But that was ere we had to bear
   The weight of parenthood!—
The cares of those we love, sweetheart,
A spice to human joys impart,
   And feed the hungry soul, my dear.

When you and I were young, my dear,
   And neither knew a care,
I trod a pathway that was clear,
   And led you, trembling, there—
But the happiness of careless days
Has broadened in a hundred ways
   Since others cling about us, dear!

WAITING FOR SOMETHING TO HAPPEN.

He grubbed away on a patch of ground,
  "Waiting for something to happen;"
Year after year the same old round,
  "Waiting for something to happen;"
The moments he had to spare he spent
  In "waiting for something to happen;"
His hair grew gray, his shoulders bent,
But he grubbed and he loafed, and was
      content
  To "wait for something to happen."

His tools wore out, and his ground grew
      poor,
  "Waiting for something to happen,"
But he grubbed and he loafed and he
      still was sure
  That "something would some day
      happen,"
And many a chance he let go past,
  "Waiting for something to happen,"
Until there came a day at last
When clods above his head were cast—
  Something had finally happened!

.

WHEN DOCTORS DISAGREE.

He looked at my tongue and he shook his
    head—
This was Doctor Smart—
He thumped on my chest, and then he
    said:
    "Ah, there it is! Your heart!
    You mustn't run—you mustn't
      hurry!
    You mustn't work—you mustn't
      worry!
Just sit down and take it cool;
    You may live for years, I cannot say;
But, in the meantime, make it a rule
    To take this medicine twice a day!"

He looked at my tongue, and he shook
    his head—
This was Dr. Wise—
"Your liver's a total wreck," he said,
    "You must take more exercise!
    You mustn't eat sweets,
    You mustn't eat meats,
You must walk and leap, you must also run;
    You mustn't sit down in the dull old
      way;
Get out with the boys and have some
    fun—
    And take three doses of this a day!"

He looked at my tongue, and he shook
   his head—
  This was Dr. Bright—
"I'm afraid your lungs are gone," he said,
  "And your kidney isn't right.
    A change of scene is what you need,
    Your case is desperate, indeed,
And bread is a thing you mustn't eat—
  Too much starch—but, by the way,
You must henceforth live on only meat—
  And take six doses of this a day!"

Perhaps they were right, and perhaps
   they knew,
  It isn't for me to say;
Mayhap I erred when I madly threw
  Their bitter stuff away;
    But I'm living yet and I'm on my
     feet,
    And grass isn't all I dare to eat,
And I walk and I run and I worry, too,
  But, to save my life, I cannot see
What some of the able doctors would do
  If there were no fools like you and me.

A RESURRECTION.

"Ah, Love is dead,"
She said;
"Flown through the open door!
Never more
While the sad winds blow
And the sad brooks flow
Shall there be
For me
The old, sweet, happy thrill—
Joy has fled.
And the world is dark and still,
For Love is dead!"

She heard a sigh,
Sweet and low!
Her heart beat high,
She forgot her woe,
And the glad wind blew,
And the sun burst through
The clouds o'erhead—
The darkness fled,
And then
She looked with joy
On the laughing boy—
For Love was alive again!

FAITH.

When the sky is blue and friends are true,
   And Fortune, fickle dame,
Bestows her winning smile on you,
   With faith you are aflame.
Then you can easily believe
   The words the preacher says,
And for your erring brother grieve,
   And join in songs of praise.

But, when the somber clouds descend
   And fortune wears a frown,
When you in vain approach your friend—
   In fact, when you are "down"—
Ah! then can you your faith retain,
   Your voice in pleading raise,
And say God's purposes are plain,
   And join in songs of praise?

THE SEARCH FOR GOLD.

The gray wolf scratches upon the door,
  While the fierce wind shrieks away,
And a woman lies prone on her cabin floor
  And a little child shouts at play.

The pine trees moan on a mountain side,
  Where a man lies stiff and cold,
And stares at the far-away stars, dull-eyed,
  And grasps a nugget of gold.

Let the gray wolf howl, let the mother
    weep,
  Let the little one shriek at the blast—
Ah, what cares he who is lying asleep,
  Has he not found wealth, at last?

THE MAN WHO HADN'T TIME.

He never had time to play,
  He never had time to rest,
But he worked away and thought of a day
  When what he had done would attest
The usefulness of his life,
  His worth as a man among men;
Then he would quit the strife—
  He would rest on his laurels then.

As a bondman chained he slaved,
  Ever looking ahead;
As a miser he hoarded and saved,
  Grudging his daily bread!
Beyond was a happy day—
  Nearer and nearer it drew—
When his work should be put away
  And care should be banished, too!

At last, upon a day,
  When the sun was low in the West,
He put his work away,
  And sat him down to rest.
But where was the dreamed-of bliss?
  And why was it now denied?
Things seemed to be going amiss—
  So he brooded awhile and died.

THE QUARREL IN THE CORNFIELD.

Up on the hill where the sweet breeze is
    blowing,
  I see the long rows of the ripening corn;
There by the fence where the tall grass is
    growing,
  Is the jug of sweet cider, beneath the
    white thorn.
And the swish of the cutters that cleave
    through the stalks,
And the song of the wind, as it blows
    through the shocks,
Come as plainly again as they did on the
    day
That I threw down the cutter and strutted
    away.

I see the big, yellow, ribbed pumpkins
    that cover
  The ground where the corn has been
    taken away—
Ah, there is a flock of wild geese flying
    over,
  Bound for some far-distant Southern
    bay,
And I hear the stern tones of my father
    again,

Bidding me go, as he coldly did then,
And again in my throat I can feel the
    lump rise,
And again the hot tears tumble out of my
    eyes!

O, for the hill where the sweet breeze is
    blowing,
  As in the fair autumn it ever blows
    there!
O, for a taste of the sweet cider flowing
  Out of the jug tilted high in the air!
O, for a rest from the roar and the rush,
From the pushing, the crowding, the
    carnage, the crush!
O, for the swish of the blades through the
    stalks,
And the song of the wind, as it blows
    through the shocks!

But the hill's far away, and the years
    have been speeding
  Some other is cutting the corn that
    waves there,
And the wind sings away through the
    shocks, all unheeding
  The pain that grew out of a foolish
    affair!—
O, for a sight of the corn on the hill,
O, for the sound of a voice that is still,
And O, for the years that have sped since
    the day
That I threw down the cutter and strutted
    away.

LOVE ASLEEP.

They builded air castles together,
 They wished by the stars in the skies,
They played in the fields in fair weather,
 And the love light crept into her eyes;
She sighed, but he laughed, and his
  laughter
Came back in sad echoes years after—
 The love light shone out of her eyes.

The maiden bound up her long tresses,
 And men praised her form and her face;
No more did she romp in short dresses,
 A woman had taken her place;
But he saw not what Love had completed,
As the boy treats the maiden he treated
 The woman who stood in her place.

One day the doves cooed in May weather,
 And a stranger looked into her eyes;
One day they departed together,
 And a boy fell to earth from the skies—
A boy with a heart that was breaking
And a love that, at last, was awaking,
 Fell headlong to earth from the skies.

THIS QUEER OLD WORLD.

It is queer how things go by contraries
    here,
  'Tis always too cold or too hot,
And the prizes we miss, you know, always
    appear
  To be better than those that we've got;
It is always too wet, or too dusty and dry,
  And the land is too rough or too flat,
There's nothing that's perfect beneath the
    blue sky
        —But—
  It's a pretty good world, for all that.

Some people are born but to dig in the
    soil,
  And sweat for the bread that they eat,
While some never learn the hard meaning
    of toil
  And live on the things that are sweet;
A few are too rich and a lot are too poor,
  And some are too lean or too fat—
Ah, the hardships are many that men
    must endure,
        —But—
  It's a pretty good world for all that.

The man who must think envies them
    that must be

Ever pounding and digging for men,
And the man with the pick would be
    happy if he
Might play with the brush or the pen!
All things go by contraries here upon
    earth,
    Life is empty and sterile and flat;
Man begins to complain on the day of his
    birth,
        —But—
    It's a pretty good world for all that!

THE RECOMPENSE.

Sometimes I wonder if the man
  Who wins renown on earth
Finds that the plaudits of the crowd
  Are of exalted worth.
I wonder if, when in the tomb
  His wasted clay is laid,
The labor and the loneliness
  He knew have been repaid.

I wonder if the common man,
  Who drifts along through life,
Content with love and praises from
  His children and his wife,
Has not less cause to murmur at
  The firm decrees of fate
Than he that frets for future men
  To find that he was great?

A FEW BOYS.

SONG FOR THE FIRST BORN.

Two twinkling stars of wonderful size
  Disappeared from the sky one night,
And these are my dear little romancer's
    eyes,
    And, oh, he must close them tight!
      Sweet little wanderer, go to sleep;
      Dear little curly head, mustn't peep—
Two sleepy eyes of wonderful size,
  And a sweet little kiss, good night!

A little white cloud had a wonderful fall
  From out of the sky, one night,
And this is his bed and his pillow and all,
  So white and so soft and so light!
      Sweet little wanderer, go to sleep;
      Dear little curly-head, mustn't peep!—
The cloud is his bed and his pillow and all,
  So a sweet little kiss, good night!

The wind sang a song to the fairies that
    lay
  Asleep in the flowers, one night,
And this is the song that is dying away,
  As fancy is winging its flight!
      Sweet little wanderer doesn't peep;
      Dear little curly-head's gone to
        sleep!—
And this is the song that is dying away
  In the dreams of my darling, to-night!

THERE IS A SANTA CLAUS.

I'm jist as glad as I can be,
  And I won't lie no more,
Nor make my mamma cry for me
  The way I have before;
I'll never, never run away,
  Nor swear again, because—
I don't care what bad people say—
  They is a Santa Claus!

Some bigger boys 'an me, at school,
  Said Santa was a hoax,
Somebody started once, to fool
  The little bits of folks;
They told me that my teacher knew
  And grandpa understood—
That your parents told you stories to
  Jist git you to be good.

Nen I went and runned away,
  And I was awful bad;
I swored a lot of times that day,
  Because I was so mad!
I'd been as good as I could be
  Since way back in the fall—
And they was no Santa Claus to see
  Or know it, after all!

But when I'd got all tucked in bed
  I heard pa say, that night,

Old Santa Claus had got a sled
   And skates fer me, all right—
He didn't know I heard him, though,
   Nen I cried, because
I'd been so bad all day, and oh,
   They was a Santa Claus!

So I got out of bed, at last,
   And climbed up on his knee,
And when he stroked my head I ast
   If Santa'd pardon me;
I told him all about how I'd
   Runned off and swored that day,
And mamma she set there and cried,
   And pa he looked away!

But purty soon he petted me,
   And after while he said:
"Well, never mind, jist wait and see—
   You'll git the skates and sled!
Those bad boys don't know what they
     say—
   Go back to sleep—for laws!
'Thout him we'd have no Christmas
     day—
   'Course they's a Santa Claus!"

THE BOY WHOSE PA HAS SPELLS.

I've jist been down with Tommy Brown
  And helpin' him to fly
A kite what his pa made for him,
  Way up into the sky.
His pa he lets him play all day
  And have the mostest fun!
He's got a goat he drives around,
  And a nawful nice air gun,
And his pa often plays with him,
  And every circus day
They go to see the show, and oh
  Wisht my pa treated me that way!

My pa he stays away some nights
  Till awful, awful late,
And so my ma she has to set
  Up all alone and wait,
And then, next morning, my, but he
  Does tear around and jaw,
And if I speak he strikes at me
  And does the same to ma,
And when he's gone ma has to cry
  Hard as she ever can—
Some day I'll take her part when I
  Grow up to be a man!

166

I guess 'at my pa never was
  No little boy at all,
For he don't never want to fly
  No kites nor bat the ball—
But wunst he stood and looked at me
  A long, long time, and I
Was 'fraid he'd whip me, so I had
  To jist give up and cry,
And then he come and stroked my head
  And didn't never speak,
But jist bent down and hugged me
  And kissed me on the cheek,
And then I cried more harder
  Than I ever cried before,
And, oh, I wisht that some time he
  Would love me so some more!

Most other boyses pas they play
  With them sometimes, but my
Pa he don't never play with me,
  Nor make no kites to fly,
And I can't go to circuses
  Like all the other boys,
And they are always tellin' me
  How their pas buy them toys,
And their pas never punish them
  Unless they're awful bad—
If my pa was that kind to me,
  Oh, wouldn't I be glad!

Sometimes when he comes home at night
  And I've been sleepin' sound,
He wakes me up and then I lay
  And hear him stompin' round,

And then, next mornin', ma she cries
    And says he wasn't well—
When I ast her what the trouble was—
    He's had another spell!—
I'm awful sorry for the boys
    Whose pas has spells, for, oh,
When his spells come he gits so mad,
    And ma she takes it so!

But if, some day, he'll only stand
    And look at me again
The way he did that first time, and
    Be just like he was then—
Oh, then, I won't care if he don't
    Make kites for me to fly,
And, oh, I'll be so happy if
    He'll only make me cry,
By bein' good to me, because
    Most fun I ever had
Was when I felt so awful bad
    Because I was so glad!

CONFESSIONS OF LITTLE WILLIE.

Pa says they ain't no spooks at all, Ni
    s'pose he ought to know,
'Cause he knows nearly everything worth
    knowin' here below;
He says 'at only fraidy calfs believes
    they's ghosts around,
For people can't git back on earth when
    you put 'em under ground.

I don't believe in spirits when the sun is
    shinin' bright,
And I can hear folks talk, or they's a
    livin' thing in sight,
If they is jist a cat or dog around me I'm
    prepared
For anything 'at comes along, and ain't
    a bit a-scared.

But sometimes I come home from school
    when ma's away, and then
I go a-sneakin' up the stairs, and then
    sneak down again,
And think I'll find the doughnuts or the
    raisins or the jam—
And then I hear somebody step—or a
    door shuts with a slam.

I know as well as I'm alive they ain't
    nobody there,

But shivers creep along my back, and I
    can feel my hair
Raise right straight up and stand as stiff
    as bristles on my head—
And I believe in ghosts in spite of all pa
    ever said.

I dassent turn around and look, for I'm
    afraid I'll see
Some big white thing without no head
    a-standin' back of me—
But after while I whistle or else I sing,
    and then
Go out and run around the yard and git
    braced up again.

And when it's dark at night, and I wake
    up and lay in bed,
I can't keep ugly thoughts of ghosts from
    gittin' in my head.
And then I hear pa snorin', and my
    blood gits froze, almost,
For every snore sounds like the groan of
    some poor sinner's ghost.

Pa says they ain't no ghosts, and I talk
    big, sometimes, and laugh
At Eddie Gray, 'cause he believes, and
    call him fraidy calf,
But when I do bad things and then am
    all alone, by Jinks,
I know they's ghosts a-snoopin' round, in
    spite of what pa thinks!

WHEN SORROWS COME.

Oh, come to me, dear little baby boy,
    come!
  Let me snuggle you close to my heart;
Oh, come, let me kiss the poor, hurt little
    thumb,
  And so take away all the smart!
      There, there, little one,
      You see it is gone,
Now, dry up your tears and away,
  For the sun is scarce up ere the night is
    begun,
So don't miss a moment of play!

Oh, come to me, dear little baby boy,
    come!
  When childhood has faded behind,
With the smart in your heart instead of
    your thumb,
  And troubles beclouding your mind—
      Oh, come to me then,
      Let me cheer you again,
As I cheer you, my darling, to-day!
  Don't sorrow alone o'er the coldness of
    men—
  And don't miss a moment of play!

GETTING TO BE A MAN.

I'm glad my hair ain't yallow,
    And all curled up and long;
I'm glad my cheeks ain't dimpled,
    And that I'm gittin' strong,
I wisht my voice was hoarser,
    To talk like Uncle Dan,
Because I want to hurry
    And git to be a man!

I'm glad the women never
    Come up to me and say:
"Oh, what a purty little boy!"
    In that soft kind of way.
I wear big shoes, and always
    Make all the noise I can,
Because I want to hurry
    And git to be a man!

I've got on pa's suspenders—
    Wisht I had whiskers, too,
And that my feet was bigger,
    And schoolin' was all through.
Wisht Edison or some one
    Would come out with some plan
To help a boy to hurry
    And git to be a man!

MEDITATIONS OF JOHNNY.

I wisht 'at I was bigger, so when I go out
 to play
With older boys they wouldn't try to
 order me away,
An' nen they wouldn't always make me
 set up on the fence,
When they are playin' circus, an' be the
 audy-ence.

I'd like to git into the ring, an' play I was
 the clown,
Or else the bareback rider, who goes
 jumpin' up and down,
Or I'd like to be ringmaster—wouldn't
 that be just immense!
But ev'ry time they make me play' at I'm
 the audy-ence.

When I git bigger, someday I'm agoin' to
 have a ring
An' be the lofty tumbler, an' clown, an'
 ev'rything,
An' then the littler boys'll have to set up
 on the fence
An' clap their hands when I perform—an'
 be the audy-ence.

A BOY'S KING.

My papa he's the bestest man
   Whatever lived, I bet,
And I ain't never seen no one
   As smart as he is yet.
Why, he knows everything, almost,
   But mamma says that he
Ain't never been the President,
   And that surprises me.

And often papa talks about
   How he must work away—
He's got to toil for other folks
   And do what others say;
And that's a thing that bothers me—
   When he's so good and great,
He ought, I think, at least to be
   The ruler of the State!

He knows the names of lots of stars,
   And he knows all the trees,
And he can tell the different kinds
   Of all the birds he sees,
And he can multiply and add
   And figure in his head—
They might have been some smarter
    men,
   But I bet you they are dead.

Once when he thought I wasn't near
    He talked to mamma then
And told her how he hates to be
    The slave of other men,
And how he wished that he was rich
    For her and me—and I
Don't know what made me do it, but
    I had to go and cry!

And so when I sat on his knee
    I ast him:—"Is it true
That you're a slave and have to toil
    When others tell you to?
You are so big and good and wise,
    You surely ought to be
The President, instead of just
    A slave, it seems to me."

And then the tears come in his eyes,
    And he hugged me tight and said:—
"Why, no, my dear, I'm not a slave—
    What put that in your head?
I am a king—the happiest king
    That ever yet held sway,
And only God can take my throne
    And my little realm away!"

SHE NEVER WAS A BOY.

When I come home, the other night,
   With an ugly lookin' eye
That I had got into a fight,
   Poor ma commenced to cry;
But when I told pa how it was,
   He clapped his hands for joy,
And told me I done bully, 'cause
   Once he had been a boy.

"Boys will be boys," I heard him say,
   "They won't be otherwise,
And the one that learns to fight his way
   Is the one that wins the prize;
When I was his age fightin' was
   My greatest earthly joy—"
But ma she kept on cryin', 'cause
   She never was a boy.

My golly, but I'd hate to be
   A girl with braided hair,
And always prim as A, B, C,
   With clothes too clean to wear!
When ma was small I s'pose she was
   Red-cheeked and sweet and coy—
But, oh, the fun she missed because
   She never was a boy!

RIDING THE OLD GRAY HORSE.

The old gray horse jogs down a way
  That leads through a pleasant land,
Where never a wrong is suffered to stray,
  And never a plot is planned!
And the breeze that blows revives and
    cheers
  And happiness fills the air,
And sweet are the sounds that greet my
    ears,
  While the horse is jogging there!

Ride on, upon the patient steed,
  As another rode long ago,
Down past the old enchanted mead,
  Where the flowers of memory blow—
Through the beautiful town of Used-to-Be,
  Which lies in the pleasant way,
And cling, as I clung to my father's knee,
  And urged the good old gray!

The old gray horse jogs down a lane
  That leads from the town of Care,
Past running brooks and waving grain,
  And meadows wide and fair,
To the glorious city of Heart's Content,
  Which stands on the hills of Joy,
And where the head of the government
  Is a shouting little boy!

177

THE FIRST CHRISTMAS TREE.

Oh, dance around it, my little man!
  Oh, clap your hands and shout!
Be merry, my darling, while you can,
  For the candles will soon burn out—
      There is care ahead,
      There are tears to shed,
  And there will be trouble and doubt.

Oh, dance around it, to-day, my love!
  Sweet faith has been given to thee—
Faith in the Glorious Child above—
  The faith that was given to me!
      But scoffers will rise,
      To "open your eyes,"
  And set you adrift on the sea.

Oh, dance around it, my dear, to-day!
  You are going to mingle with men,
And the faith that you have will be taken
      away,
  And gloom will encompass you then!—
      Till your own little one
      Sends care on the run,
  And brings the old faith back again.

THE GOOD NIGHT KISS.

I saw a sweet young mother place
    A hand upon her darling's head;
A blush of shame o'erspread his face,
    As lovingly, she said:
        "Come, dear, 'tis late,
          You mustn't wait,
So say good night, and go to bed."

He looked at me with sheepish eyes,
    And softly tried to steal away;
I thought of one in Paradise,
    Who taught me how to pray:
        "And must I miss
          My darling's kiss?"
I heard the fond young mother say.

Her cheeks were round and soft and fair,
    As were another's long ago;
I saw a child with sunny hair,
    O'er whom a mother bended low,
        I heard her say,
        As he fled away:
"And pray for the orphan, too, you
    know."

I sigh for the clasp of a tender hand,
    And the kiss that a shamefaced boy
    forsook!

I sigh for the love he could understand
  At last, when they bade him "come and
    look!"
    But a boy never knows
    Till the fond eyes close,
  And the Lord, in his wisdom, shuts the
    book.

A BOY'S COMPLAINT.

Almost the last words father said
  To me before he fell asleep
Were: "William, keep this in your
    head:
The crop you sow you'll have to reap!
Don't envy others what they've got,
  But you just do the best you can
For all the world, and you cannot
  But grow to be a worthy man."

I've had to work since father died—
  I've learned a lot I never knew
Before he went; but still I've tried
  To do the things he told me to.
I've never cheated anyone,
  I've always tried to shun the wrong;
If he can see, he knows I've done
  My level best to help along.

But every day or two I meet
  Someone that father used to know,
Who says: "My gracious! It does beat
  Creation how these boys do grow!"
And so he stops and looks at me,
  And I could knife him then, because
He's sure to say I'll never be
  Quite such a man as father was.

A week ago my Uncle John
    Came on a visit from the West;
"Gosh, how you've grown since I've been
      gone!"
    He said—and then I guessed the rest.
He grabbed me by the muscle—gee!
    What an awful grip he had!—
"But o' course," said he, "you'll never be
    Quite such a feller as your dad!"

Still, mother tells me not to care
    What such unthinking people say;
She says she knows I'll make them stare,
    If God but lets me live, some day;
"For even Washington," says she,
    "No doubt was often sad because
Folks told him he would never be
    The man his humble father was."

www.ingramcontent.com/pod-product-compliance
Lightning Source LLC
Chambersburg PA
CBHW031107020726
47495CB00007B/2086